Ghar Vapsi

AN ILLUSION

Udit Kumar

INDIA · SINGAPORE · MALAYSIA

ISBN 979-8-88805-477-2

परिंदों को मिलेगी मंज़िल यक़ीनन ये फैले हुए
उनके पर बोलते हैं; वो लोग रहते हैं खामोश
अक्सर ज़माने में जिनके हुनर बोलते हैं।

This world is the reason that forces him to hide from his true himself. People around him treat him like an *invisible* object and make him feel that he hardly exists in this world. Initially, he tried his best to prove himself and showcase his ability, but this failed to make any considerable impact. So, finally, he decided to lock himself in his self-created cage. His fear provided more and more strength to the bars of his cage. He sat in a corner there, keeping his head bowed and waiting for his moment to come. A moment when he would not have to justify himself, that day, he would like to stand on a cliff and shout as loud as he could and disclose all his weaknesses, fears and worries to this world.

A bit later, a sudden thought changes his mind... he can see the faces around him start to turn towards him with insulting smiles and millions of fingers pointing at him like the whole world is trying to pull him down. With every passing second, his breath becomes more laboured, so he closes his eyes and enters his self-made, cosy, happy, imaginary world. This world comprises all the things that he desires or dreams of all the time. Since he follows and loves his world so much, everything here is designed and defined minutely, so much so that it is a parallel world in his subconscious mind—where it is very convenient to live—and the people in his world never disappoint him. This is the world made up of characters and stories in which he overcomes different scenarios made up as per his convenience providing him with a precious feeling of success.

Contents

Prologue

'I' is the most isolated word defined by literature, experienced by humanity and always denied by nature (*since nature is always driven by a chain in which each component is dependent on another for its existence*). Even God has realised the pain behind this 'Un-habited' word, 'I'. Hence, He created emotions, feelings and love. This helps fill the emptiness and creates each person with his or her multidimensional characteristic.

Right after the birth of a child, the character starts to develop. Every small lesson a child learns involves the moulding of the nearby ecosystem. This is the core nature of human beings, which will be part of his/her future character. This moulding comprises types of people, their habits, the languages they speak, the tone they use to express their words, what they eat, including how and when they eat, their festivals and the ways they are celebrated, the types of jokes or methods to express their emotions, how they treat their elders, talk to their little ones and millions of other things.

These aspects were not developed by a single human being or a generation. It is the summation of the life led by our ancestors and their changing habitats. All these changes are continuous but happen very slowly *to be adopted by a* single human being. The adaptability of human nature to these constant changes makes us rule this planet and proves us superior to all species.

Now, let us recall one incident from our childhood, which I believe all of us might have experienced. We may remember the first time we tried to run down a slope. During the first few moments that we start running, it would feel fantastic, as we need to put less effort into running than usual, and as our speed gradually increases, so do our level of happiness. We realise that we are running our fastest without putting any effort as we proceed further. But very soon, a moment comes when we realise that our rate has now reached a dangerous level. We try to reduce our speed immediately, but the situation is not in our hands anymore. Our feet carry us forward uncontrollably. At that moment, our body, feet and mind do not coordinate and ultimately, we fall.

If we analyse the above activity, we realise that our body is ready to adjust to gain stability against acceleration. Since the mind has confidence, the body will follow its instructions and make us feel happy. But we do not realise that the body has limitations when acting against any **rate of change**. Even our mind fails to give any kind of warning before the body reaches its breakpoint.

This is the only reason that even after facing continuous changes in the last 3.4 million years, humans have reached this scenario today, starting from the Stone Age. We should not forget that these 3.4 million years made us adaptable to these changes; otherwise, we would have become eliminated. A high rate of change is a hazardous sign for an individual or the whole society. This should always be considered to avoid damage before reaching our breaking point.

And in this race of development, we have created a society with **two different groups of people** *where one* section manages to change with time. At the same time, somehow, one group cannot keep up with the pace laid down by the other and, after a while, this causes a massive imbalance in terms of social, economic and political differences.

'Inequality in concentration in terms of the social, economic and political platform can never construct a stable society.'

What does science say?

It is impossible to keep these two different sets of people apart within society. Society merges and averages out both these groups. This merger will result in a collision and hence, instability. And do not even think about overcoming this situation by strengthening a single group because this will naturally develop the other group in the same proportion and ultimately increase the impact of the collision.

A simple example can illustrate this situation. Look around us. Notice the criminal cases happening in our society, especially incidences like rape. If you think this crime can be minimised or eliminated by strengthening the law or increasing the number of police officers around you, then I am sorry, but you need to think again. Rather than wasting our effort to strengthen the barrier between these two different concentrations, why not put our energy into equalising the concentration of these two different worlds to eliminate the barriers between them?

Chapter 01

Introduction

"I am going out now. You know I am travelling today," someone whispered in my ears. Obviously, annoyed by the disturbance, I shifted to one side of the bed but could not make out the owner of the voice in my sleepy state.

After a few seconds of silence, I think the other person understood this and said, "Arya, it's dad."

I suddenly turned over in my half-asleep state and looked at him. He wore black trousers, a white shirt and a navy-blue tie. He looked ready for work. One could tell from the facial features that he was my dad because I resembled him.

When I realised that he was staring back at me, I said, "Where, Dad? You didn't tell me about this..."

"Oh, son. I did," he interrupted me. "I told you I would be travelling to Bangalore to attend a conference. Just that the date got shifted at the last moment and I have to go today, or I will not be able to address their concerns," he explained.

"Oh, I see..." I said, rubbing my eyes with both my hands. "When will you be back, then? I hope it will be soon because if you remember, we have a PTM (Parent Teacher Meeting) in our school at the end of this week..." I said with a catch in my voice.

"I remember, son. It is on Saturday. But unfortunately, I won't be back before Monday," he said.

"Dad, I have been reminding you about this for the past month. What are you going to do now? Because Mom already said that she wouldn't be available and you know my class teacher..." saying this, I covered my face with the blanket.

"And Dad... It's a Sunday today!" I said suddenly, moving my head out of the blanket.

"Oh, yes. But you know, the conference will start tomorrow at nine am and early-morning flights are unavailable. These aviation companies never miss a chance to increase the fare when it's required urgently," he explained.

"But Dad, Mom is also going to Pune today, as Shalu Mosi is admitted to the hospital due to dengue. What will we do alone at home for a whole day?"

"I don't think you and Vishnu will miss such an excellent chance to spend time with your PlayStation. I believe you will qualify for stage 3 today. Be patient and don't empty your weapons early like always. And the most important thing is, don't forget to take care of your sister. If you need anything, call the maid or Sunita aunty. I have put the money for your school project on the dining table. I have also added both of your monthly allowances. I hope everything is settled now," he said.

"Everything is settled, sir!" I said with a smile. As dad bent over and gave me a big hug, I was pulled out of my negative thoughts. I reciprocated and then he pulled away.

I lay back on my bed watching him leave. I rolled over to check the time on my alarm clock, which showed five o'clock. "I still have an hour and a half to sleep," I murmured and closed my eyes.

As I closed my eyes, I could hear mom and dad talking and the sound of the door creaking a moment later.

Let me introduce myself—I am Arya Singhal, a 15-year-old living in Bombay with my mom (M/s Supriya Singh), dad (Mr Ashok Singhal) and my 6-year-old little sister (Asha Singhal).

My dad was a project consultant. His job required frequent travelling, sometimes even up to a week. My mother was in the IT sector. Usually, she is back home from her office by six pm but may become late four or five days a month. Mom defined them as 'hectic days.' My wonderful little sister studied in my school in the 2nd standard.

The name of our school was Global Heritage School and we used to travel by bus. Mom helped us get ready and prepared our lunch and breakfast while dad walked with us daily to the bus stop in the morning. After that, mom and dad used to go to their respective offices. When we returned from school, the maid would prepare our evening snacks and sometimes help Asha to complete her homework.

Vishnu was my classmate and lived in the neighbouring flat with his big, happy family. His apartment was just in front of ours. We were friends and his family loved my sister and me. When mom and dad were not home, we spent a lot of time at his house. His parents and dada and dadi were amazing. His father was a teacher at a nearby engineering college and used to get back from college by 5.30 pm. Vishnu's mother was a housewife.

I do not know why, but some comparisons were always happening in my head regarding Vishnu and his family. If anything happened in our house or to me, I always wondered what would happen if the same thing had occurred in Vishnu's life or his family. Maybe it was because that was the only family with whom I was so close. To give you the details, since our family had two earning members, we were more financially stable than Vishnu's family. We had a maid in our house while Vishnu's mother used to do all the housework. My dad owned a brand-new Fiat car, while Vishnu's father had a scooter. On my last birthday, dad gifted me a video game, which he purchased from the US while he had gone there for some office work. Our house was full of decorative things, especially pottery, as my mom loves them. Every weekend, when she had the time, mom painted them. We were often soundly scolded if they broke due to our games.

In the morning, my mom was always in a hurry, sending us to school and preparing our lunch and dad's breakfast. When she came back in the evening, she prepared our dinner. So, most of the time, our home was not tidy. It was clean, but things were always lying around, here and there.

Usually, dad came late in the evening and sometimes late at night. That is why we hardly met 2–3 days a week in the evening. But yes, he used to drop us off daily at our bus stop in the morning. Other than Saturdays and Sundays, those were the only ten minutes we interacted with each other.

In Vishnu's house, everything was well managed. Everything, though not decorative or expensive, was kept in its designated place. It looked average but beautiful. His father spent more time with the family. Their family's best moments were in the evening when they all sat down together on their balcony and had tea. They would laugh loudly while conversing. Vishnu's father knew the names of all our teachers and the subjects they taught. He knew everything about our school activities. Vishnu even told him about the punishments and fights in our class. He used to come to the PTMs. His mother helped Vishnu complete his project work, took mock tests before viva and discussed many minor things with him before the exam, which might have appeared childish but I saw them as an empty gap in my life.

Vishnu's dada and dadi were the cherry topping of their family. After their dinner, they would go on an evening walk almost daily. I used to watch them from my bedroom window and imagine I would also spend quality time with my family one day.

Chapter 02

The Life

In order to achieve more and more speed in our life, we are not ready to remove our feet from the accelerator. Yes, most of us put extreme effort into getting promoted or moving ahead to improve our financial standing and career growth. All this is a crucial part of our journey until we have a clear vision of our partial, in-between or ultimate goal. A race without a finish line can never be completed with utmost satisfaction. Believe me, none of us wants to finish our life with a feeling of having failed relationships, missed opportunities and having made poor judgement calls. Some choices seem easy at the time and later turn out to be poorly informed; others are difficult from the beginning.

Remember, investing our extra effort in one place means ignoring the other part of life. This ignorance or gap can be filled only if it is for a short period. Ultimately, we need to maintain balance in life. Without this balance, nothing will be stable and, in the end, the different dimensions of our life will be affected.

We cannot ignore the common feelings people have in the last few moments of their life.

I wish I had spent more time with the people I love.

I wish I had worried less.

I wish I had forgiven more.

I wish I had stood up for myself.

I wish I had lived my own life.

I wish I had been more honest.

I wish I had worked less.

I wish I had cared less about what other people thought.

I wish I had lived up to my full potential.

I wish I had faced my fears.

I wish I'd stopped chasing the wrong things.

I wish I'd lived in the moment.

We should not forget the limitation of our minds. Our rate of change of pace should be monitored by the brain. Otherwise, things will get out of hand without any warning and could result in severe consequences.

The most important thing is to reach our destination or even a satisfactory level from where we had started. What is the problem or shame in decelerating ourselves, taking a moment to feel and enjoy what we achieve? Try to regain that lost balance in our life and change our preferences for a short time.

Why are we programmed to win each and every battle?

Why do we want the tag, 'successful' above our heads?

Remember, by the time we succeed or win in our life, half of the businesses around us would not be able to earn their multi-fold profits. Most companies around us want to uplift our lifestyle and make us feel like achievers. In exchange for this, they will put a hole in our pockets and place an extra burden on our shoulders. Ultimately, we have to run fast behind virtual and fabricated traps while leaving behind the real things around us.

This is because they have conditioned our brains to connect their products with our status. Hence, they make us feel that only successful people use this and their product will differentiate us from others.

Ultimately, we will be stuck in a vicious cycle. The faster we run, the more complex it will become. Finally, it will lead to an uncontrollable speed and an un-balanced life.

Yes. 'Life: The most beautiful game designed by God.'

We say that our fate was sealed when we took birth and had not even opened our eyes; God had already decided everything. We just need to play the role and follow the path that He has set for us.

Do you ever think about what went through His mind when assigning us a role in His game?

He, who could make every living being happy, could provide us with a life without any problems, never make us cry and does not want to be partial to anyone. But this can never be defined as life.

Life is like food that can only be made tasty or edible when it has all the ingredients in the right proportion. Overdose of anything can affect its nutritional value as well as its taste.

Hence, to avoid all this, He provides us with feelings, the power to think and emotions so that we can react to ourselves and put together our own recipe. Because he wants us to live, not the fate that he has decided for us.

Let us understand this with an example. When you are sitting alone under a tree and you see a group of ants moving in a line carrying some objects, you often try to change their path, distracting them with a stick, sketching a line between them.

Do you know why?

It is not like you want to hurt or kill them. It is because of your curiosity, not cruelty. Knowing how they will react to the disturbance introduced by you is simple. What will they do when you sprinkle water drops on them? Either they would run away or keep on moving in the line.

God does the same with all of us. He has set the field, given us some targets and included different scenarios. When we start playing, he keeps adding obstacles to our life. It does not mean he wants to hurt us but is always keen to know how we will react or overcome those obstacles.

Those obstacles could be either in the form of happiness or pain.

And all these things are overall defined as Life.

Chapter 03

A Misfired Diwali

That morning, dad came home from his official Delhi conference after three days. Since it was Diwali in two days, we were all home. I was playing with Asha in the living room and mom was busy in the kitchen. I did not know exactly what, but something did not sound right between mom and dad.

He slept throughout the day and went to the club in the evening without saying a single word to anyone. Asha and I guessed it was the club because he had taken his club identity card from the side pocket of the fridge before leaving.

For the last six months after his promotion, he was always running from pillar to post, never taking time off to be with his family. Mostly, when he returned from his conferences or meetings, he spent his time outside the house. Asha and I were very excited, as Diwali was in two days, but dad's behaviour spoiled everyone's mood. That day, he came home drunk from the club. Since it was eleven pm, I was semi-awake and Asha had slept. I could hear dad falling in the living room, the noise of something getting broken. After that, I could not figure out exactly, but an argument between mom and dad could be heard for over half an hour. In the end, that conversation ended with the door banging and it looked like dad slept in the living room while mom slept in the bedroom. I closed my eyes and prayed to God to make my family more like Vishnu's. I could not understand the tension between my mom and dad.

I mean, I could not figure out what was causing all this. We had all the necessities in our house. I did not know why dad was constantly under pressure. If there was some issue beyond my knowledge or understanding, we could have coped by doing away with all the unnecessary things around us, deciding with whom we wanted to compete or what we wanted to achieve.

Around that time, I started to imagine life in Vishnu's house. It was clear that resources were much less in his house, but there was a stillness in his home. All the family members talked to each other and if someone was under stress, they were always concerned about the person. After their dinner, they used to stay put, just laughing, talking, joking or even arguing. Moreover, there was a sense of togetherness, showing a feeling of deep attachment.

My mom always tried to handle things; she made sure we were unaware of dad's behaviour. However, most of the time, her to-do list after office used to be so long that she would get frustrated and even start shouting nonsense at us. Sometimes, in her anger, she would mention dad's irresponsible behaviour. During all this, a lot of the time, I could see her hiding her tears.

Dad used to go for a walk daily at five am. The next day, I wanted to join dad; it had been a long time since we talked and I did not want to miss the opportunity. In the morning, I woke up with the alarm. I came out of the room and saw dad sitting on the chair in his tracksuit, wearing his sports shoes.

From behind, I put my hand on his back. He turned around and said, "Good morning, my *beta*... You woke up so early?" with a bit of surprise and humour in his tone.

"Dad, can I come with you for the morning walk?" I said, rubbing my eyes.

"Of course, *beta*. I've always asked you to come with me. Get ready and wear a jacket or sweater. It's cold outside," he said, massaging my head softly.

After some time, I came out of the bedroom wearing my sports shoes and jacket. Mom and Asha were still sleeping. We went to the nearby park. It had a charming jogging track with trees and grass surrounding it. In the morning, the whole park was covered with mild mist and the grass had dew drops. Walking on the grass gave me the feeling of someone spraying water droplets on my feet from beneath. The weather was a little cold but comfortable.

After a few minutes of silence, I said in a high-pitched voice, "Dad, tomorrow is Diwali. Please try to stay home. We will have so much fun together. Do you remember last year, how Asha was afraid of crackers? This year she is excited and waiting to dance under the fireworks. We will decorate our balcony with colourful lights like last year, and in the afternoon, we can go shopping."

Dad quickly figured out that whatever I said had been thought-out and he looked at me with a little smile.

Tugging his hand, I continued, "Please, Dad, let's do the same this year, too."

He replied by flickering his eyes and squeezing my hands. I was hoping that he was indicating a 'yes' by this. Again, we started to walk.

After some time, I murmured, "Dad, you have changed now," and I stopped. Dad held my hand and we sat on a bench next to the jogging track. He put his hand on my shoulder and said, "I can understand, dear. For the last two years, I have been busy with never-ending work. So, I could not concentrate on both of you. But I love you a lot." His voice was heavy as he said this.

"You know, when we shifted to Bombay, we came with just two bags of clothes. Before that, I had a job in Lucknow. Your mother had completed her post-graduation after our marriage and you were just a year old. When we shifted here, the first few months were miserable. Your mom and I struggled a lot to make ends meet for the three of us. One night, you had a 104^0 fever. I can't forget that dark night. It had been raining since morning. No autos or taxis were available. We waited for two hours. Your mom started to panic. We used to have a Bajaj scooter and finally, we decided to go by scooter. Your mom was holding you in one hand and an umbrella in the other. This way, we reached the hospital. Because of the heavy rain, you got wet and were shivering badly. After meeting the doctor, we changed your clothes and decided to stay in the hospital. That whole night, your mom didn't sleep for a single second. She wrapped you tightly so that you would not get cold. That night, I decided to put all my effort into giving my family all the happiness in this world. Money and resources will never be a hurdle for my children."

With this, dad's voice started to break and I could see tears in his eyes. I stood up and hugged him. Slowly, he whispered in my ears, "Don't worry, son, we will celebrate this Diwali better than the last one." After this, he turned his face and started to walk pulling on my hand. Maybe he did not want me to see his tears.

I do not know why, but I had wanted to unburden myself to dad for a long time. Many questions kept floating around my head, so it seemed the perfect time to me. At any cost, I did not want to miss the opportunity. Somehow, things did not seem settled to me. I sat down on the track and looked down. At first, dad asked me, "What happened?" But then he sat down beside me.

"You know, Dad, I understood your journey when I visited our Dadi's house. I could see that all our relatives and family were still way behind us financially. Nobody prospered as much as you and I can understand completely. It's never easy to start things. Today, when I look around me, I do not think we lack anything. Dad, for the last 2–3 years, I have observed a difference in our house. I can remember earlier we used to have less stuff. Just a funny example, Dad, do you remember the items we used to have in our bathroom? A bathing soap, shampoo and toilet cleaner!

But in the last three years, unexpectedly, these three have multiplied into thirty. These items have become a vital part of our life. You know, Dad, using all these items is a luxury, but it hardly contributes to the happiness level in my or our life. I just wanted to make a simple point, whatever extra effort you are putting in to include this stuff in our life can be given up if all these can be converted back into time spend with us. And this will add more value to all of our lives than any other thing could. I do not know much about our financial status, but comparing our day-to-day life with Vishnu's, I can only say that we have enough. What is the use of all this if it is not serving its ultimate goal? Now it's time for all of us to enjoy these luxuries together. Honestly, Dad, I am terrified sometimes when I imagine the direction our life is leading to. You know, in the last few years, Mom has also changed a lot. After seeing all this, Asha keeps asking so many questions, but unfortunately, I do not have any answers for her. Please, Dad, you are my hero. You taught me so many things in life, especially to be independent. Let's give a new direction to our family before it's too late."

I still had many things to say to him, but my throat clamped up refusing to speak. I started crying loudly like a child. I could hear dad make a sobbing sound. A few people in the park observed this and they stopped for a while to watch us, but then moved on.

I just could not explain how relieved I felt after that monologue. We moved towards the water tap in a corner of the park, washed our faces and started towards home.

Dad played with us that day and we watched a movie after lunch. Then, in the evening, we went to the market for Diwali shopping. It was after a long time that we had all gone out together. Even though mom and dad were not talking to each other, we had a lot of *masti*. At the end of our shopping trip, on Asha's demand, we had ice cream. It was some real family fun.

The following day, dad woke me up. The clock showed that it was six am and dad was wearing his formal clothes with his usual trolley bag. Before I could say anything, he started, "Son, something very urgent has come up in the Bangalore office. Last night, we had an accident on a site there. So, I can't cancel my visit. I will return by evening. I know Diwali pooja is at eight pm. I will return before that."

I could not say anything. I kept staring into his eyes. I shook my head, seeing him leave the room and went to sleep again.

Asha woke me up at 7:30 am. She had a nasty habit of pulling my ears and nose while waking me. It was very irritating, but as I woke up and looked at her naughty smile, all my irritation vanished and converted into a big smile. I dragged her onto my bed and she started shouting, "Mom, *bhaiya* is beating me..." Then she said, "Freshen up. Mom made your favourite poha and banana shake. If you are late, I will finish yours too." Saying this, she ran out towards the dining table.

When I reached the dining table, mom and Asha were already there. The poha and banana shakes were arranged on the table and smelled delicious. I was a little surprised to see the extra plate, but before I could say anything, mom asked me to call dad for breakfast.

"But, Mom, he left for Bangalore at six am. Didn't he tell you?" I asked. Mom ignored me while moving towards the kitchen, trying to hide her expression, murmuring something under her breath. So, I tried to neutralise the situation and said, "Mom, it was urgent. He said he would return before eight pm, before the pooja."

Mom did not reply and the two of us started our breakfast.

It was 7:30 in the evening and Diwali pooja was going to begin at eight pm. Mom and Asha looked fabulous in their new dresses purchased the day before. They were busy arranging the items for the pooja. Asha was decorating the temple with flowers and rearranging the lights with intense concentration. Vishnu and I were organising our crackers and planning their sequence.

I tried calling dad; his phone was not reachable. "Maybe he still hasn't landed," I thought. Finally, at 8:30 pm, his phone started to ring. Dad picked up and said, "Hey, son, I just landed at the airport and will reach home by ten pm. Just about to board a taxi."

"But Dad, we are waiting for the pooja," I replied, sounding a little worried.

"I am sorry, son, the flight was delayed. You start the pooja. I will join you later to burst the crackers," he replied.

While talking to dad, mom was looking at me mutely. She sat down to begin the pooja with Asha and started chanting the mantra. I also sat behind her. After the pooja, we lit *diyas* all over our home, then moved to our society's park with a bag full of crackers. Vishnu and his family were already there. We lit a lot of crackers and had fun. It was good to see Asha burning an *anar* (a multicolour firecracker) without being afraid. All of us then danced under it.

Meanwhile, Vishnu's father ran toward us and warned us not to go near the firework while they were burning. It was a lot of fun and we were laughing out loud, but I could figure out the pain my mom was hiding behind her fake smile. Once Vishnu's mother asked her about my father, she replied laughing, "He will be late due to some last-minute work."

Vishnu's dada and dadi were sitting on a chair at one corner of the park and watching all of us. After a small photo session with his family, we returned home, a little surprised to see dad sitting on the balcony and watching us from there. Nobody said a single word. As soon as we entered the house, we could smell whisky on his breath. After some time, Asha went to dad and started telling him about the crackers and our other activities. I entered my room to change my clothes and go to bed. Taking a long breath, I pulled up my blanket and fell asleep.

Chapter 04

A Visit to Paradise

Anything in this world can be justified. Good and bad or right and wrong is just our point of view. It will not be justice if we start to expect that our point of view will be accepted equally by everyone.

This is because our point of view on anything depends upon many unpredictable factors like its impact on our life in the current situation, our knowledge about the issue, our relationship with the other person, our character and other factors like our social and economic status.

I am writing all of this because my narration about my father or my family might appear negative. Still, I am writing genuinely about what I saw, felt and observed according to my ability to understand and follow events.

Later, when I visited my dada and dadi in Lucknow, my perspective took a sharp turn.

This visit to Lucknow was exceptional. After a long time, we visited them together, with a relaxed schedule and no particular task to be completed. Considering the situation in our family, it seemed like a pretty great opportunity for us to return to happier times. Even during our journey, I could sense some kind of silent clash between my mom and dad. Asha also noticed it and asked me, but I ignored or diverted her questions as best as I could.

Let me introduce my dada and dadi and the beautiful moments we shared with them. My dada is Mr Dharmendra Singhal and my dadi is Mrs Devki Kumari. Dada retired two years ago from his state government job and is the most satisfied person I have ever seen in my life. He was very calm and did not depend on any external factor for his happiness. He spent most of his time supporting my dadi's daily routine. Dadi was a housewife and had all the qualities of an ideal grandmother. She was very caring, emotional, clear about her daily routine and very precise with its sequence. Life here was different compared to our Bombay routine. In Bombay, most of the time, we were rushing and, in a hurry, to complete our daily tasks, while here in Lucknow, situations or tasks were executed in slow motion. Schedules were present, but many small things were also considered, which were simply ignored in Bombay. I do not remember a single time here when all the members were not present at the time of breakfast or dinner. It was compulsory for everyone to be present and the routines were followed on priority as per dadi's rule book.

Multiple times, dad was late for dinner. Then, she would keep calling him, even scolding him, but she would never serve dinner without him. Dinner had a different definition here. Our evening meal, called 'dinner' in Bombay, usually lasts 20–30 minutes. But here, it could extend up to two hours, in which everyone had to describe their whole day, plans, schedules, tell jokes, pull each other's legs, discuss our Bombay neighbours, our relatives and more.

After dinner, we would feel thoroughly satisfied in body and mind. During this time, we would exchange so much information with each other, that we could explain what was going on in each other's minds. All this gave us a kind of satisfaction and made us feel affectionate towards each other.

Dad was being cared for like a small child by dadi. She often made him dishes, his favourites (most of them we had never heard about). She would also narrate a short, exciting story or incident related to the same. Usually, all these stories would end with a burst of enormous laughter from us and a look of embarrassment on dad's face.

Dada sometimes shouted at him and he would be silent with a charming expression on his face. It was very pleasing to see the drastic change in dad's role from "Man of the house" (in Bombay) to "child of the house" (in Lucknow).

Many times, in Bombay, when dad used to get very upset or stressed because of his workload or after some argument with mom, he would say that after my and Asha's education was completed, he wanted to settle in Lucknow. After experiencing life here, his thoughts could be justified and were no longer a surprise to me.

Dada and dadi started their day with their morning walk at around six am. It was not a regular walk, they walked with their separate groups of uncles and aunties. Surprisingly, most of the time, the gap between these groups would be almost 100 metres. Their murmuring voices contained discussions, complaints about their daily routine and updates on their health. It lasted for around one hour and then both of them would return home.

Then, dada would come to our room and wake us all, except mom, as she used to wake up before they came back from their morning walk. When mom saw dada and dadi entering the house, she would start preparing morning tea for all of us. Meantime, after dada's first call, if she had not woken up, he would come inside and pick up a sleeping Asha. As for dad and I, we would have already woken up. All of us would sit on the first-floor porch, surrounded by small plants. All the plastic chairs were arranged in a circular formation, with the tea kept at the centre. This tea session usually extended up to an hour accompanied by discussions on our daily schedule. Sometimes dadi told us an exciting story about dad's childhood or some related story. My dad had been very naughty in his childhood. Dadi told us how his tuition teachers used to scold him often and neighbours came home to complain about him. After all this, dada would also punish him severely. But all these never stopped dad and he kept repeating his antics periodically.

Meanwhile, Asha would have woken up completely, she would get down from mom's lap and perform two recently learned poems. We would applaud her efforts. I could not imagine a much better start to our day than this. We had more than 100 plants in our house. As part of the daily routine, dada and dadi would provide nourishment to them, remove dead leaves and then wash each and every plant individually. It was our assigned job in the garden to water them. Asha and I would water our small garden outside the house using a hose; dad would wash dada's car and scooter while mom got busy in the kitchen preparing our breakfast. Often, after Asha and I finished the garden, we would join dad and help apply shampoo to the car. We would enjoy ourselves a lot and, in between, splash water at each other. Sometimes, dad would also play with us, but if mom saw us, she would shout from the kitchen window, come outside and pick Asha up as she would be entirely wet.

After our joyful, allocated work was done, it was time to take a bath, as dadi was very strict about this. Breakfast would not be served until everyone had finished their bath and all this was followed by a small pooja ceremony attended by everyone. At breakfast, we would list all the pending jobs and distribute them among all of us.

One day, after the extended breakfast, dad and dada went to the bank for some work, while mom and dadi were engaged in the kitchen cleaning up after breakfast and preparing lunch. Both of us were responsible for refilling the water pot and the seeds jar kept on the terrace to feed birds. A small portion of our rooftop was designated explicitly for the birds and magical things used to happen here. When dada came here after his breakfast to feed them, hundreds of birds would already be waiting for him. Upon seeing him, they would not fly away; they would give way for him to reach the centre. Some of the birds would dip their beaks in the polythene. On dada's other hand, there would be a bag full of seeds. With this, dada would point them in the direction where he was going to throw the seeds. Meanwhile, the group of birds would remain in order. It was very normal to dada and dadi, but it was a spectacle to us. Sometimes, a squirrel or two would come from somewhere and enter the group of birds, but dada would shout at it, "Can't you wait? I brought a special gift for you today. Why did you come alone today?" While dada's facial expression would not be funny at all, you could figure out that his reaction was as if he were communicating with some of his close friends. Then, he would take some groundnut from his pocket and throw them toward the squirrel(s). Surprisingly, only the squirrels would react; none of the birds was interested.

Another day, dada promised that in the evening, we would all go to the market together. As per his early promise, we could buy a bicycle for Asha and a smartphone for me. Dad tried to oppose it, but it was useless in front of dada. For the first time, I realised that even dad could be overruled. Dada outargued him with solid reasons and, finally, everyone agreed. Asha and I had already worked out our gifts. We had finalised the brand and colour long ago and waited eagerly for the evening.

We went to the market in the evening to buy our gifts. Dadi purchased some clothes for mom and dad. After that, we went out for dinner in a restaurant even though dada and dadi were not very interested in restaurant food. Dadi suggested, "We should try something different today. One of my friends told me that this restaurant serves delicious curd rice."

Dada did not seem very convinced, but took a deep breath and replied, "As you wish."

Initially, dada praised the dish, but on reaching home, something funny happened in the kitchen. Secretly, in a low voice, dada requested dadi to prepare something for him, as he had not liked the food in the restaurant and was feeling hungry again.

Dadi came to our room, murmuring in anger, "I am totally responsible for this habit of his. Your Dada, not even a single time, adjusts to outside food. Now at ten pm, he expects me to prepare food for him."

Dada replied instantly, "Then why did you order curd rice there? You know I don't like it at all. And these guys charge like they are bringing the curd rice straight from South India."

Dada continued, "I am telling you; you can open a nice restaurant here; at least those guys will learn what real food tastes like."

Dadi murmured something and went inside the kitchen.

This was the beautiful, emotional rhythm between dada and dadi, which we noticed very often. Their bantering brought vibrancy to their relationship. They always focused on the moment without thinking about the future. I had never seen them hold on to their anger. The tremendous hidden love in their arguments could be felt quite easily.

We laughed and went to our respective rooms.

I was busily customising the settings of my new phone while Asha removed the plastic wrapping from her bicycle. At this moment, dada entered our room and asked me if I wanted to come with him for a walk. I agreed and went out with him. The weather was excellent. After inhaling the Bombay air, the air here seemed much fresher. The roads were empty and silent, which was not what I was used to. Asha also followed me to the main gate, but mom took her back. After returning from the market, she had not even changed her clothes. After dada emitted a few satisfying burps, we started walking. He broke the silence, put his hand on my shoulder and asked, "So, what have you decided to do after your 12th class?"

I said, "Dada, I am confused, but planning to join mass communication at some good university." Anyone could have figured out the lack of confidence in my words and so did dada. He understood my confusion, but I could see the calm smile on his face which was there most of the time. After a few seconds of silence, he said, "See, *beta*, it's not essential which line, stream or career you choose in your life. Ultimately, what matters is whether your chosen track can carry your dreams smoothly, fit in with your goals and whether you like it. For example, being a doctor, engineer or sportsperson should not be your ultimate goal. The most significant thing here is what you want to achieve after being a doctor or an engineer. You should decide your motive behind choosing any profession, but earning money cannot be set as your primary goal. If you aim for money, you'll never be happy because you always end up wishing for more. It's a toy that you'll get bored of soon. Your ultimate aim should be to do something that makes you happy and will keep you comfortable in the long run, not only for now but in the coming years too.

And many times, I've observed people your age get distracted looking at successful people or trendy careers or jobs. They always try to run towards that transient fame and glory they see trending around them. But never forget that every single person is different and has unique characteristics. And, of course, everyone comes from different circumstances and backgrounds.

See, you must understand the difference between value and price. Just take an example. Let's say I give you ₹10 and assign you a task that should be utilised to its maximum. Now ₹10 has the same value worldwide and for all individuals. But it will be best utilised when it's spent with maximum impact. This means that its value could change depending on the circumstances. Imagine a person dying because of hunger. Then, this ₹10 could be a lifesaver for him and you will be equivalent to God's messenger to him while another person could have zero value for the ₹10. If you offer him the same, he will consider you a fool since this amount will hardly make any difference to him.

Every person on this earth starts their journey from a very different platform and different circumstances. So, the same job could be a lifetime achievement for one and a symbol of failure for another. It's not about the job but its value to the person doing it. And this ultimately defines the true definition of success that will be directly dependent on parameters like where you started, what you dreamt of and under what circumstances you have achieved it. Maybe you reached there after succeeding, but another may have failed and fallen to the same level.

So, comparing things based on their price is a most foolish thing. Just analyse the value based on your situation and then decide whether you would accept or deny the same.

To understand your social position, you must know the history and journey of your family. There were many steps, decisions taken by many people that ultimately created the situation where you had the opportunity to study in a world-class international school in one of the major cities in India. If I start with my dad's generation, then as you know, he did not have any electricity in his house till he turned 50 years. The entire family depended on limited resources produced by farming. There was neither road connectivity nor any school in that village. Despite that, my father had a vision that his son would not live this life. So, with his support and my will, I completed my studies. For the next ten years, I worked as a helper in a tiny firm located in Delhi, but I continued my education and finally got a government job. Even after that job, life was complicated. Your Dadi and I couldn't even imagine that we could afford a house in a city like Lucknow or ever get the opportunity to sit in a car.

Then your dad came and you know, right from his birth, I decided that I would never let money come in the way of his dreams. Resources would never become a hurdle for him, but in return, I never expected any extraordinary thing from him. From his initial student days, he was average and surprisingly, he maintained this intermediate level consistently till his last day of education. During this period, he often got involved in fighting and cheating, got some complaints from his tuition teacher and once I even caught him in a restaurant with his girlfriend, your mom. But all this never hurt me or made me feel bad. I sense some sort of responsibility in his eyes all the time.

These responsibilities are not a burden or any kind of requirement from you. It's just a token of love and blessing from your ancestors, which are being transferred from one generation to another. And you must not forget that these blessings are offerings and an integral part of you."

"Arya!" Dadi was shouting from our main gate. We were standing around 100 metres from there.

"Yes, Dadi. Coming," I replied. It was 11.30. I started walking towards the house with dada.

"I remember when your dad was your age, I explained this sort of thing to him too," dada murmured something inaudible and I could see a smile on his face.

When we reached home, everybody had already fallen asleep.

I think most of us live our lives just considering the tip of the iceberg, never thinking of the vast base holding up that tip. Even a single thought in our mind is not instantaneous; it is the summation of millions of invisible but valuable things we carry with us. None of this is in our control. As rightly said by dada—these are the blessings—carrying the fragrance of our ancestors, the summation of their thoughts, their living style, their struggle, their strengths and their weakness.

Chapter 05

The Monster

When you think that you have started to understand some very complicated situations and things are starting to be under your control, then from nowhere, a storm comes and blurs your vision. When you open your eyes, the circumstances have changed. Every decision has backfired. You seem to be thriving in a sad and lonely atmosphere. The situation is entirely out of your hands and you only have the memories left with you.

You are helpless, just helpless!

As if God is not happy with you and is punishing you for the deeds in your past life.

It is remarkable what planning and thought it would have taken for God to sow the seeds of life. It was evident that humans were not our planet's first life form. It all started with midget algae. After years of transition, we came into existence. But for every form of life, there were plenty of obstacles to be faced and the test starts from the time of birth!

Sometimes, I think about how impartial God is. Impartial, not in the sense that he created the rich and the poor, the fit and the diseased, and the beautiful and the ugly. By impartial, I mean the power to think and the presence of emotions that every human on this planet has. Every person faces obstacles in his/her life. The magnitude changes from person to person but what actually matters, in the end, is how a person tackles his/her problems.

It may be that a child born in a posh family, playing in a golden cradle with a safe and secure future faces problems. Not financial, but circumstantial, emotional and family tension throughout his/her life; he/she will curse God while dying despite having lived all his/her life in affluence.

However, a child with a dark future, even when in his/her mother's womb, is an added responsibility to his/her slum-dwelling family. He/she lives a peaceful life, has a caring family except for financial issues and thanks God while bidding adieu to this world.

It does not matter where you were born or what you had when you opened your eyes to this world. What matters, in the end, is how you overcome the obstacles God sets in your way. The rich may get overconfident and become self-indulgent while the poor overcome all the obstacles cautiously and, in the end, emerge the winner in the race of life! This shows that there is a wide gap between birth and death with God's planned obstacles, which we alone have to fill. How one fills the gap decides one's fate. Nothing is destined to happen in life. How we make our effort count and how we use the precious gift of intelligence provided by God as a tool decides how we leave this world—with repentance or with pride!

The following day, after our pleasant and well-established morning schedule, we were sitting around the dining table, just having finished our breakfast and discussing some random topics. We had a return flight to Bombay in two days. It was hard to believe how the last seven days had flown by. As always, as our return date came closer, a kind of despair started to fill us up. Often, dada used to say, "Good times travel faster than the difficult ones." This visit was very special to me, maybe because

I could understand everyone in-depth this time. I realised that in the last few months, I had developed a better perception of people and was figuring out unspoken words and unexpressed emotions in every situation.

Dadi and mom were busy discussing packing and compiling the list of various things that dadi normally sent with us when we return to Bombay. These items included homemade pickle, ghee, dad's favourite laddoo, Asha's favourite mouth-watering rasgullas, and mine and mom's favourite special salty snacks prepared by dadi. They had already started making all these items the day before. Asha's birthday was on 30th May, four days from then, two days after we left Lucknow. That is why dada and dadi scolded dad for planning our schedule thus.

Dadi said, "We could have celebrated her birthday here if only your dad had planned this trip in a better way. Sometimes all these nonsense emergencies are indeed difficult to understand."

Dad had already clarified that he had an important conference in Bangalore that he could not afford to miss. Also, Asha had her monthly test on 29th May. But somewhere, dad knew that it was impossible to beat dada and dadi with all these arguments. Before dada could take up dadi's case, dad ran inside the bedroom and, within a few seconds, came back carrying something in his hand. It looked like it was some paper that he was trying to hide behind him. Watching this rare action from dad, we were all perplexed.

I could not resist and asked, "Dad, what is this..." But before I could complete my sentence, dad shouted like a child, "Surprise! Indeed, we can't stay till Asha's birthday, but both of you can come with us and be a part of the grand celebration there!" Saying this, dad handed over two sheets of paper to dada. Holding the papers, dada murmured, "Our tickets to Bombay." Everybody looked at dad with their mouths open, as nobody was expecting this kind of dramatic performance from dad. Asha broke the silence and started to clap. Within seconds, everybody joined her. But dada interrupted and, looking at dadi said, "But it is not possible, as we have to go to my friend's son's marriage the day after tomorrow." Before dada could conclude his sentence, all of us started to shout, "Dada, please *na*... Dadi, you tell Dada to come with us. It will be great fun." Dadi replied, "Oh yes, how could we miss such a great opportunity... We will celebrate Asha's birthday together." Dada did not look very convinced but did not say anything, indicating that he agreed.

Meanwhile, Asha climbed onto the dining table and started dancing in front of dada, which finally brought his trademark smile. Dada picked Asha up from the dining table. Dadi quickly picked up an empty plate from the dining table and said, "Now, wrap up everything fast. We have double targets and very little time left for our packing and other preparations."

Before dadi finished this alarming statement, we stood up from our chairs. Dad hugged dada and kissed Asha's forehead, saying, "This year, my angel will celebrate the best birthday of her life."

After this beautiful surprise from dad, everyone's excitement level peaked. A few minutes ago, while planning our return journey, everybody was hiding gloomy feelings inside, but dad magically converted them into happy ones.

Our flight was on the same date and from the same terminal but with a two-hour difference. We reached Bombay airport and waited for them. When dada's and dadi's flight arrived, dad booked two taxis and we returned home. I was very excited to tell Vishnu about our fabulous trip, eager to show him my new phone, and of course, about this surprise twist from dad. Mom looked a bit tense as we had left our home in a mess while leaving Bombay. In the taxi, dad told us that he had already booked our society community hall for the birthday party. Dad had taken care of the catering, food menu, guest list and other preparations well in advance.

He even invited most of the people without informing us. Dad had given me the responsibility to choose and order the cake before the event. When Asha heard the word "cake," she came to me and shouted, "It's my birthday, so the cake will be my choice." Dad asked, "Okay, little princess, please tell me your choice." Asha replied, "The chocolate cake should be two-layered and the theme should be from Mickey Mouse, like it was there at Aradhya, my classmate's birthday party." We laughed hearing such a specific description from Asha. The party was more elaborate than we expected. Dad had invited most of his office colleagues, people from our society and friends. I could even see most of mom's office and kitty party friends.

It was a gathering of more than 400 people. We clicked photos with dada and dadi and posed for a family photo, followed by many selfies with dadi and Asha. Surprisingly, dada and dadi performed a few dance steps to some old Hindi songs. For the last few minutes, dad and Asha joined too. Everybody was clapping and having fun. I saw Vishnu standing in the corner with his family, so I dragged him onto the dance floor and asked him to dance. He was very emotional, hugged me with tears in his eyes and whispered in my ear, "Great dear, I am so glad to see your family together and enjoying so much; I wish things would be the same all the time."

I went to the DJ, requested him to play our favourite song and started dancing with practised steps (once we had performed together in school to the same music). At eleven pm, the guests began to leave. According to our society's rules, the music system was also not allowed after 10:45 pm.

At last, only Vishnu's family and we were left. We finished dinner together. Then, all of us walked back home. Asha started counting and guessing her gifts and was excited about opening them. Dad had a conference the next day in Bangalore, so he had his flight at seven am. While setting his alarm for 4:30 am, dad observed that Asha was planning to open her gifts at night. He convinced her that since it was already 12:30 am, she could open them the following day with dada and dadi. It was a difficult task, but she finally agreed and with this, the happiest day of my life ended. I was so pleased. Whenever I tried to close my eyes, all the pictures accrued since our visit to Lucknow would replay in my mind in a kind of slide show. I had a big smile on my face.

Whenever I remember these moments, the echo of this laughter will always play in my heart.

I covered my face with a pillow and finally managed to sleep.

At 4:30 am, with the irritating sound of the alarm ringing, I woke up. I pushed my face out of the blanket and observed that dad was getting ready. Usually, his travelling bag remained packed and parked in one corner of his wardrobe. I got out of bed and saw dada and dadi sitting on the balcony and having tea. After half an hour, dad touched dada's and dadi's feet, kissed my forehead and put his hand on Asha's cheeks while she was sleeping. Mom had already prepared and packed his lunch. Then, he sat in the taxi already waiting in front of our building.

The previous day, mom had promised that we would take one day off from school and spend an entire day with dada and dadi as they had a return flight the following evening. Mom had to go to her office, but she said she would return early that day. From the moment dada and dadi had come to Bombay, they were a little uncomfortable because of the drastic change in their daily activities, as they had a set routine. They tried to replicate it with the limited resources at hand here. In the morning, they used to go for a morning walk alone (without their chit-chat group), then water the 2–3 small plants on our balcony. Then, dadi helped mom in the kitchen. While dadi continued in the kitchen, mom got ready for work and would take her bus to the office.

It was 9:30 am. After finishing our breakfast, dada tried to call dad's number several times, but it was unreachable. I told dada several times, "Maybe the flight got delayed, Dada. Air India has a reputation for delayed flights. You never know for what reason they might have delayed their flight."

During our dinner with Vishnu's family the previous night, I had introduced dada and dadi to them. At that time, they had invited dada and dadi to their house for lunch the next day. So, we started to get ready for lunch at 10:30 am. Several times, dadi asked me whether they were vegetarian or non-vegetarian. This was the first time that dada and dadi were visiting a Maharashtrian family for lunch. Dadi mentioned in the morning that she knew from her TV serials that Marathi people ate fish or seafood daily. However, my dada and dadi were pure vegetarians. Dadi told me that once when dad was in the 10th, dada had caught him eating eggs outside our society. After that, dadi gave him dinner on a paper plate and scolded him badly.

I told dadi, "Don't worry, Dadi, Asha and I eat at least 5–6 times a week in their house." Dada looked a little surprised but smiled at me.

Dada bought clothes for Vishnu as a gift. During all this, Asha was walking around with the single agenda of opening her presents. She had already started to unwrap them and created a complete mess in the drawing room. We decided to help her and began separating cloth boxes, money envelopes and other household gift items. Asha was disappointed after seeing these, as she was only interested in toys and games. After seeing a flower pot in one box, with a hilarious expression, she looked at dada and said, "It's my birthday. How could they even think of choosing this sort of present for me? Didn't they find any toys in the shop?" Hearing this, all of us started to laugh.

It was two pm and dadi told me to collect all the open boxes and gift wrappers so we would not be late for Vishnu's house. While we were about to leave, the doorbell rang. Vishnu was at the door and had come to call us for lunch. He had also taken leave from school for that day. Dada was still in his room, I ran to call him, but he was busy on the phone. After seeing me, he said, "Your Dad's phone is still unreachable. Why is the flight so late?"

I smiled and told him, "Don't worry, sometimes he switches his phone off while attending any conference or web meeting." But dada replied immediately, with a concerned voice, "But how could he be so irresponsible? He should have called once he reached there."

I replied, "We are late, and see, Vishnu has come to call us." We reached Vishnu's house and his family greeted us very warmly. Vishnu's father was not there as he was at his college. After a quick round of light snacks, lunch was served on the dining table while dadi went to the kitchen to help Vishnu's mom. We started to play in his room and then we had lunch together. Dadi enjoyed the unique flavours of the food prepared by Vishu's mom so much that she noted the recipe of many dishes and promised to try to make them at her kitty parties in Lucknow.

After lunch, all of us sat together. Due to the vast cultural difference, everyone was interested in listening to the different dimensions of the conversation. At five pm, Vishnu's dada insisted on us having tea. But somehow, dada convinced him to allow us to leave as they had to finish packing and leave the next day. After dada and dadi invited all of them to visit Lucknow, we came back to our house. I called mom and asked her, "Did you speak with Dad? His number has been unreachable since morning."

Mom replied, "I have also been trying to call him since morning but, no use. Maybe he is busy with his conference. Don't worry! I have the number of one of his colleagues from the Bangalore office. I will call him and will confirm the same." With this, mom hung up the phone.

Meanwhile, dadi made tea and banana shakes for us. After a few minutes, dada's phone started to ring; it was mom. Dada's phone had a high speaker volume. Most of the time, a person sitting nearby could hear the conversation very clearly.

Dada picked up the phone and I could hear mom say, "Papa, I called his Bangalore office and some of his colleagues. They are saying that there was no meeting planned in Bangalore today and Ashok was not expected there. After this, I called his Bombay office and even his boss. They said Ashok had been on leave for the last ten days. This means he hadn't joined his office after we arrived from Lucknow. But Papa, he has been going to the office for the previous two days." With this, mom's voice started to rise.

Dada tried to control the situation. "Don't be afraid, *beta*. Perhaps there is some confusion. He has a client-based job. Maybe he is busy with some of his clients in Bangalore without keeping his other colleagues in the loop. Please don't panic and be calm. At what time will you leave your office today?"

Mom replied, "I am on my way and will reach in 15–20 minutes."

Dada replied, "Okay, come home and then we will figure this out."

With this, dada hung up the phone and sat on the sofa nearby. We were listening to the conversation. Dada asked me to bring him some water. I went to the kitchen and got a glass of water for dada and dadi. Meanwhile, dada tried dad's number continuously, but it was switched off.

Dada told me while finishing the water, "Check the status of the Air India seven am flight online." Then, in between, he paused and asked me to switch on the laptop. We opened the Air India website and started to track the flight, but there was no trip displayed in their schedule for seven am or around it for Bangalore. Then we called Air India customer care. They confirmed that they had no flight before ten am to Bangalore. Now the situation was becoming more complex and intense. All of us tried to hide our anxiety, but it was evident in everyone's facial expressions.

Meanwhile, the doorbell rang. Asha ran towards the door. It was mom. She rushed inside the house and sat on the sofa next to dadi and said, "I called all of his friends. Nobody has any clue about him. Most of them said that he is on leave due to our Lucknow visit and then for Asha's birthday preparation."

Dada very calmly explained the conversation with the airlines. After this, mom could not hold her tears and started to cry, but dadi came to her and held her shoulder. "Don't worry, *beta*, it's just that Dada is impatient. Just wait, he will come. Maybe his phone got stolen or battery drained."

Then mom interrupted, "But Mummy, in that case, why did he lie about the office or flight schedule to us? I remember yesterday evening before the party, he mentioned his office activities for the day and then told me about today's meeting in Bangalore. I remember precisely because, due to this visit, we had to prepone our ticket from Lucknow to before Asha's birthday."

While saying this, she put her head on dadi's shoulder. Asha was standing in the corner of the living room trying to figure out the situation. I picked up mom's handbag and brought a glass of water to her. Meantime, dada was trying dad's number continuously. Mom went inside her room. After 10–15 minutes, she called dada and me inside. When we entered her room, she was working on her laptop, checking online transactions done from dad's bank account. She pointed me to an address and a doctor's name and number written on a notepad. She placed her hand on my shoulder and said, "This hospital is in Dadar. For the last three days, your dad has been making a payment there in the morning. Go there with your Dada and try to figure out the reason."

While mom was explaining this to us, dadi was listening, standing at the room entrance. Then dada said, "Get ready, while I arrange a cab to Dadar."

Within 5–10 minutes, the cab arrived. We got in; everyone came to see us off. We tried to control our emotions. During the journey, I asked dada thousands of questions, but he tackled them all positively. I was trying to divert my mind as best as I could but was imagining the worst possible scenarios. It was around 8:30 pm. By this time, traffic had reached its peak; it took us two hours to get to the hospital which was fifteen km away. We confirmed the doctor's name from the receptionist and rushed to the doctor's cabin. He was sitting in the room and attending to some patients.

"Hi, doctor," I said. The 50–55-year-old doctor, wearing thick spectacles, was surprised to see us enter his cabin directly in a hurry. He replied, "Hello, dear. How can I help you?"

Dada stood next to me and said, "Doctor, it will be a little strange to you, but we have come here to get some information. I am the father of Mr Ashok Singhal, who has been visiting you for the last few days."

The doctor was familiar with dad's name, which was clear from his facial expression. Before dada could ask anything further, the doctor interrupted him and asked us to wait for a while outside his cabin as he was attending to a patient.

After a few minutes, the patients left his cabin and he called both of us inside. While indicating to both of us to sit on the chairs next to him, he said, "Yes, I've known Mr Ashok for the last five years. He has been coming to me for yearly medical check-ups. We collaborated with his company to conduct routine check-ups for all of their employees. So, I meet him once or twice a year." The doctor looked at my dada and asked him to be patient since he was going to say things directly and to the point.

"Last year, he came to my hospital in November–December for a regular medical check-up. During that time, he complained about some minor swelling in his throat. After the primary examination,

I recommended several medical tests. His reports detected throat cancer, but it was in the initial stage and curable. There was a simple course that I strongly recommended Mr Ashok complete immediately. It was for three months and included some therapy and medicines followed by routine tests. But there was one necessary condition—if the sequence broke, all the procedures must start from the beginning again. Even after two attempts, we were not able to complete the course. According to him, due to his busy official schedule, he could not manage the time. He ignored it entirely and made things worse for himself. By closing your eyes, you may skip the problem momentarily but cannot prevent it. For the last four months, he had not visited me at all. Even after many follow-up calls and warnings from me personally, he didn't respond or contact any other doctor. Last month, his throat hurt badly for two days straight. The nightmare awakened. Initially, he thought the pain would go away, but it grew stronger until he couldn't take it anymore. He returned to me and underwent an x-ray and the other required diagnostics. The monster had awakened again in a more severe shape. A big black spot proved a truth that was difficult to believe. His cancer had reached the final and incurable stage. He confirmed the reports in other hospitals, but the results were the same.

We sent all of his reports to various international practitioners for their consideration, but everyone denied the possibility of any cure at this stage. The day before yesterday, I called him to discuss those responses and to return his reports. After a long conversation between us, he revealed that initially, he had even considered suicide. But he couldn't after imagining the reactions of his family, whom he loved the most in this world and who still didn't know this truth. He often mentioned that he didn't want to suffer in front of you. He hardly has one month left. Very soon, he will start to show severe symptoms. So, he decided to move away from all of you. He handed over this bag that contains all his reports and some personal notes for his family and asked me to hand it over to you whenever you came to me. And yes, finally, he mentioned that he is going away from everyone and that you shouldn't try to find him. He wanted to live his last moments alone and didn't want to share his pain with his loved ones. I tried to convince him that he should stay with his family in the last moments of life, but he looked very determined about his decision."

With this, the doctor stopped and made eye contact with dada while holding his hand. After listening to all this, I froze. I could not breathe, and it felt as if my heart had constricted.

The whole situation felt like a dream. My mind just stopped giving me any instructions. I turned and looked into dada's eyes, which were filled with tears. I stood up and hugged him, started to cry, sat on his lap and for the next 10–15 minutes, I did not say anything.

Dada broke the silence and, in a broken voice, asked the doctor, "Why didn't you stop him or inform his family about this?"

"I tried. I tried contacting his office to get the family's number. I even got a landline number from there, but it said it was out of service."

"How long does he have?" dada asked.

The doctor replied, "His cancer has reached the last stage and spread all over his system. It is hard to tell. It depends upon the patient, but hardly a month. And very soon, he may lose his voice as his vocal system got damaged due to the spread. I am sorry to say, but he will need his family in this condition."

I hugged dada tightly with one hand and held the bag in my other. The next moment, my phone started to ring. At first, I could not figure out that it was my ringtone. Then, the doctor picked it up from the table and slowly showed it to me. 'Mom' was displayed on the screen. The next second, I snatched my phone from the doctor. Then, I started to shout as loud as I could. I sat on the floor and tears began to flow out of my eyes as if some dam had opened up.

Many people came inside the doctor's cabin and gathered around us. The doctor gave me a water bottle and said, "Be strong. Your family will need you at this crucial time." Then, he looked towards my dada and said, "You should go home now. My driver will drop you and if there is any way in which I can help you at this crucial time, please let me know. I will be available."

Dada was not reacting at all, just sitting quietly and looking outside the car's window while holding me with one hand. I could not hold my tears and asked dada, "What will we do now?" He did not react in any way.

Finally, we reached home. It was 11.30 pm. Mom opened the door and started to shout as she saw me.

"Why did you not pick up your phone? I have been trying continuously for the last hour. It was switched off from then!"

I ran towards her and started to cry as loud as I could while hugging her. Before she could ask anything of dada, he also broke down and started to cry out loud. After a few minutes, he explained everything the doctor told us. But mom said, while holding her emotions, "I can't believe this bullshit from that stupid doctor."

Saying this, she grabbed the bag the doctor gave me and turned it over. Many medical reports and a diary fell on the floor. I picked up the medical reports and opened them one by one. All of them were from different hospitals and addressed to dad. Meanwhile, mom picked up the diary and we sat down to read it together.

Chapter 06

Risk Assessment

Imagine how these crowded cities look from a few hundred metres above the earth's surface. It will be similar to ants running all over the place before the rainy season in search of and accumulating food for the upcoming crucial period. But we humans act more wisely and have eliminated this requirement from **a period** to **all the time.** As a result, we keep running in a hurry to accumulate all the materialistic things of the world in our ant mounds (homes) our whole life.

We are stuck in this endless race and never bother to evaluate how much to collect. We are busy running and running and running.

In between all these, we learn the fantastic term 'competition,' which means other people should not be ahead of us no matter what. This competition teaches us to accumulate more things, of better quality than others. And in case we failed to do so then, we will either consider ourselves a symbol of failure or put more effort to get ahead of them.

Just look around and figure out why people are running all around. Have we ever thought about why they do so? Suppose we want to understand this on a broad scale. In that case, we can conclude it as 'All the effort that a human being is investing from his/her birth till his/her last breath is for the single agenda of making their and their loved one's lives more comfortable, secure. To prepare himself/herself against any upcoming possible risks.'

Now the question arises, to what extent is this security or preparedness required? (That is, preparing ourselves against any risk or the comfort level we want to achieve).

#<u>Risk assessment</u> 'Identifying and analysing future events that have the potential to negatively impact individuals and their assets.'

Risk assessment is necessary for every individual to identify and define how many levels an individual needs to be prepared for possible upcoming risks in his/her life. All this will help us plan our earnings and investments and ultimately define our current workload. All our evaluation is based on individual past experiences, society, family members, social environment, goals in life and other similar factors. It is not at all necessary that the risk assessment of any two people will be the same. But before this, we need to understand the difference between **possibility** and **impact**.

Consider the example mentioned below.

- A terrorist attack—The psychological impact of these particular events is deep-rooted in our minds. Often in a public place like a railway station or airport, if we see anything suspicious, all the previous stories that we have heard related to terrorist activities start to replay in our minds., but examine the possibility of the occurrence of this event in our life.

* In 2018, approximately 350 people lost their lives due to this.

(High Impact and Low Possibility Event)

- While taking the example of a road accident, the possibility of occurrence is far more than we can imagine, while the impact can be understood against the below data.

* In 2018 alone, 1.5 lakh people lost their lives due to road accidents. Followed by countless permanent and severe disabilities.

(High Impact and High Possibility Event)

- In 2018, the World Health Organisation (WHO) predicted that one in every ten Indians will develop cancer and one in every fifteen will die of the disease. Even the detection could significantly impact an individual and his/her family.

(High Impact and High Possibility Event)

- Most of us have an extra sense about protecting our children. We often hear from people around us that their main aim of earning is to secure their children's future. So, this has a significant effect on our minds. But just imagine, apart from investing in children's education, will our money help them secure their future? Even after proper training from us, they would not be able to manage. And if they do not, then with our extra support, are we making them strong or crippling them?

(High Impact and Low Possibility Event)

Our priorities should be based on the possibility of an event occurring. This means that we should be well prepared for the crisis with the highest probability of occurring, while the impact is to be considered a state of mind, like an individual's past experience, family background, financial backup and relationship with their spouse or parents.

The question could arise here, What is the problem with building an extra layer of protection for ourselves or our family? But remember, to gain this extra protection, we may have to sacrifice our present happiness.

Sacrifice does not only mean the loss of something from our end, it indicates an imbalance that we create in our lives due to our extra effort to earn money or unnecessarily secure things with a very low probability risk. This will directly or indirectly impact all the people around us and there may be a chance that we may not give enough time to our children today because of this imbalance. To fill this gap, we will feel the need for more money later, just because we did not react at the right time.

The above statement can be easily understood as a widespread practice people follow nowadays. To earn money or to achieve a specific level professionally, we initially work like animals and ignore our health. Then, within a short period, we spend this extra earned money to restore our health. Looking at today's scenario, it is more probable that we will suffer from a lifestyle disease.

Observe the traffic around us. The probability of an accident happening is much higher. Instead, we lose our jobs one morning and, despite our skills and ability, cannot earn the basics for our family. Lack of self-confidence is the primary factor forcing people towards securing additional financial protection.

That does not mean that we should not be prepared at all. Of course, we should have a backup, but it should be precise and well-calculated.

Now, the second component is 'comfort.' Again, this also depends upon the individual and thousands of other factors, but we need to consider the following point.

Just look around us and consider whether all the accessories around us are really required. Analyse for example our bathrooms and list down all the accessories we have there.

Soap, shower gel, shampoo, conditioner, hair oil, body lotion, moisturiser, hair gel, toothbrush, toothpaste, tongue cleaner, mouth wash, hand wash, hand towel, bath towel, toilet tissue, hair dryer, toilet cleaner, tile cleaner, cleaning brush and then a few more things related to shaving, cleaning, manicure/pedicure kits, beauty products, etc.

Now we need to understand the strategy of the marketing people behind all these. They create more and more requirements and develop new segments every day, which relate to the social status of the consumer. It is a trap.

Can you imagine the role of the floor cleaner, toilet seat cleaner and bathroom tiles cleaner being so specific that they cannot be sold together as a single product like it was done before? It is the same with shampoo, conditioner and moisturiser. I am not raising any questions about the efficacy of these products. My only point is to evaluate them against our extra effort to earn enough to afford them.

Just because of some strategically created need, we work like animals, sacrificing the precious moments that can be spent with our family and friends. If these moments are appropriately invested, then we could produce some real happiness around us.

But we always choose to get promotions and increase our income so that we can spend money on useless things and ultimately the companies can convert their millions into billions. Finally, we need to consider whom we want to impress by showing our expensive houses, cars and the decorative items around us. We do this by reducing our valuable moments with our loved ones, hiding our mental pressure/tension all the time and converting our relationships into volatile things.

Chapter 7.0

The Real Pain (Letter from Dad)

Sorry for not saying goodbye to you all!

Sorry for making you face this scenario!

Sorry for being an imperfect husband and dad!

Sorry I did not have enough time to be with you!

I know no words in the language could express my feelings and justify my actions. But one thing that I wanted to convey to all of you is that you are the best part of my life. I love you all above everything in this whole universe.

Yes, whatever the doctor told you is true. I never had the courage to explain my disease to you. I cannot even imagine seeing myself waiting to die in front of you. Initially, I was waiting for some miracle to happen, but they simply do not exist in the real world. Now, I realise the value of every second that I wasted on nonsensical, virtual things. I could not reveal my true love to all of you when I had the opportunity. Look at this tragedy, the moment when I was about to reach the phase of my life where things were getting settled, they were about to be in my command, everything suddenly collapsed like it never existed. It ultimately proved me wrong and weak in every aspect.

Now, with every passing second, minute and hour, time is dragging me down, trying to squeeze me. With each of my collapsing breaths, I started to feel like I was melting down and dissolving into the soil. Just look at the joke played by God; it's the same soil I never gave any priority in my life, even when it was always there with me, under my feet.

Life is a game of ups and downs. Some valleys are worse than others. Unfortunately, I made you all face the giant canyon in your life. But the harsh truth is that none of us is ever immune from tragedies. It is easy to count our blessings when riding on top of those hills. The accurate measure of a person, I believe, is when you can still see the grace you have while travelling from the mountains to the valley.

Always remember, no matter what you go through in your life, big or small, you are incredibly blessed. When facing a challenge, focus on your blessings and hang on to them tight.

This letter will give you strength and make you realise what I learned during my journey in life. I must hand over all my learning to you. Otherwise, my struggle and hard work will lose their purpose and content.

I do not want you to repeat my mistakes. I want you to learn from them. I want you to start your race from the point I left and not waste your time and energy on doing the work again. You should not have to learn from the same mistakes because I already did.

Of course, the scenario I am facing now could not be predicted by anyone. All of these are a part of life and are not in anybody's control. But yes, things could have ended in a better way, or God knows, could even have been eliminated. It is now a complete waste of time to discuss the different possibilities or scenarios that could have occurred to avoid this situation.

Before starting, I wanted to let you know that I am thankful to my father, always. He allowed me to ride on rough roads alone, taught me to fight, allowed me to fall and gave me the courage to stand without any support. Though he was always there, I could see the pain in his eyes every time I fell or failed. He always expected me to develop my point of view to see this world. He even let me pick my future direction. He once told me, "Good or bad times in life depend on several unpredictable factors, but they should be based on your decisions and choices."

Son, you have to learn things in multi-directional and more profound ways. Do not be unduly influenced by anyone or follow anything blindly.

My motive is not to influence you but to give you an idea of how a situation can vary if we analyse it from a different angle. You are not supposed to follow my path blindly. You just need to understand the circumstances, realise the mistakes, utilise my learnings and use them in your life whenever necessary. Dear son, at this point, your role is crucial since you are responsible for your mother and sister. Before making any decision, ensure that you constantly analyse the impact on their life.

Being a mother is a difficult job; believe me, being a working mother is probably the most challenging job. I witnessed how your mother struggled tirelessly every day with a smile. Consciously or subconsciously, I learned countless life lessons from how she handled our life on a day-to-day basis and, in return, willingly or sometimes unwillingly, she supported every decision I took and secretly provided me with the strength to see it through. That is why you can find her reflection in every action and thought during my journey.

I promise that one day, you will need these bits and pieces of advice, so tuck them away in your heart and draw them out whenever necessary. You are always an incredible blessing to me, your mom, your sister and of course, to this world. You are meant for great things, son. But remember, the greatness of these 'great things' must be defined just by you. No one else should be there to decide what its limit is, what would be great for you, or what magnitude would be enough for it to be called 'great.' And believe me, I cannot wait to see how you make your mark on the world.

Chapter 7.1

Love at First Sight (Letter from Dad)

Now, you should understand the journey of our family from the beginning. With this, you will get an idea about the circumstances and reasons behind my various decisions, which ultimately led to the end of my journey.

After dad's transfer, when we shifted to Lucknow and our truck was unloading, we did not even have our water connection ready. Dad told me to bring some water to drink from a neighbour. I did not know anyone there, so I ran towards a random house adjacent to us, pressed the doorbell and a girl aged between 18–20 years came out. She was tall and had slightly curly hair tied up in a ponytail. A few of her hair fell next to her ears. She had deep black eyes, fair skin and tiny round gold earrings. She was beautiful.

I introduced myself as her new neighbour and asked for some drinking water, pointing to the jug I was holding.

Meanwhile, an old lady, maybe her grandmother, came out shouting, "Supriya, you first finish your lunch!" Momentarily, before she turned and went inside again, the grandmother pointed her finger toward me and asked rudely, "Who are you?"

I replied with a slight hesitation while pointing towards my house, "We are shifting here today, so I need some drinking water." Surprisingly, she asked the same question again, "So, who are you?"

This question confused me a bit. I paused and replied softly, "Sorry, I don't understand what you mean."

She raised her voice a little and asked, "Caste?"

"Oh, sorry, I did not get that. We are Chaudharys," I replied.

She took the jug from my hand and went back inside her house. Her facial expression seemed like she did not like my answer. After some time, she returned with the jug full of water. She asked me again with a sour expression, "You mean Jaat (an agricultural caste group in north India)?"

I replied, "Yeah."

Then, I returned home, absolutely delighted by the thought that such a beautiful girl was living in our neighbourhood.

After settling in the new city, my next big task was to get admitted to a reputed college. I started my research and listed all the colleges offering BBA courses with their cut-off marks. Since I was not an extraordinarily brilliant student and had scored 65% in my 12th, only two colleges were available for me to choose from. I filled up their forms and started preparing for the entrance examination. Luckily, I got admitted to my first choice of college.

One day, I was returning from my college after completing all the necessary formalities for admission. It was a bright afternoon and I was walking near the house. This is when I saw that pretty girl again. I tried to remember her name but failed.

She rode a bicycle, wearing a yellow top and a white bottom. She looked absolutely gorgeous. To my surprise, she looked at me and started to come toward me. I stopped there and continued to stare at her. It took her a few seconds to cross the street and come to the side where I was standing. During those precious long seconds, my heart was pounding like it was going to explode, break my rib cage and fly out into the air. A hundred thoughts must have crossed my mind in those seconds. I wondered if she was coming toward me to talk to me. She passed me and entered her house. For some time, I stood there and observed her while she entered her home and parked her bicycle. I felt like a creep but could not resist admiring her beauty.

After that day, the moment I came out of my house, my eyes would automatically turn towards her house and search for her.

Subsequently, I joined college. I did not know anybody in my college or the city. During lunchtime, I was sitting on the stairs alone, watching some boys playing football. Suddenly, I looked upwards and saw the pretty girl again. I did not expect her to be there at all.

She was walking towards me. Initially, I was horrified, thinking maybe she had noticed me while I was staring at her that day. But another part of my mind was going crazy, realising that we were in the same college. She reached and stood in front of me.

I acted like I had not noticed her and turned my face towards the football ground again.

She said, "Hi, you remember me?"

Before I could decide what to say, she continued, "Oho! Remember that day you came to my house for water?"

I blushed and shook my head with a dumb and confused expression, "Oh, wow... Great to see you."

"So, what are you studying here?" she asked, smiling.

"BBA Today is my first day here. And you?" I replied.

"Great, I am in BBA too. Second year," she said.

Then, somebody called her from behind, 'Supriya!' She turned away and said while leaving, "Okay, bye!" and ran towards the group of girls standing to one side of the football ground.

This conversation made my first day of college remarkable. Whenever I came out of my class, I kept looking for her. I even asked for the location of the classroom for second-year students. When the day ended, I got back on my bicycle to go home. It was boiling out there as summer was at its peak. The distance between college and home was around 4–5 km. I was sweating a lot.

At that moment, I realised that someone was repeatedly shouting 'Hello!' Initially, I ignored it, but as I turned around, I saw that it was Supriya. I slowed down. She was on her bicycle and her face was almost red due to the heat.

She said, puffing, "How fast you ride. I was calling out to you, but you seem to be lost in yourself."

"I am sorry, I didn't expect anyone to know me in this new city," I said. Our bicycles were very slow and parallel now. She said, "I forgot to ask you your name."

"Ashok," I replied with a goofy smile on my face.

We rode on, discussing the college, faculty and random topics for the rest of the journey. Her smile refreshed me, overcoming the effect of the hot weather. Every moment of that day is still fresh in my mind. Even today, I could draw her picture perfect if I had the skill.

When I reached home, mom and dad asked me about my first day in college, but I was in a different mood. All the conversations with Supriya kept floating around in my mind.

Our conversation was not awkward at all. It was not laden with any flirtatiousness. The connection between us was utterly unspoken, but something special was there (at least from my side). Supriya seemed very bold and open-minded. It seemed that during our conversation, I was more cautious than her.

I was eagerly waiting for my second day of college to begin so that I could see her again. The following day, I got ready at 8.30 am sharp, even though I had to leave for college only at nine am. Mom and dad sensed some abnormality as I repeatedly took a round of our gate to figure out what time she would leave. It was 9.10 am. By now, mom was losing her patience. She came out of the kitchen, stopped me while I was going towards our main gate and said, "Your classes are supposed to start at 9.30 am. Why are you still here?" Before dad heard this and asked further questions, without replying, I took my bag and left the house on my bicycle.

I rode hardly fifty metres from my house when I saw Supriya coming out of hers. Mom came outside to close the gate, but I was unsure whether she noticed anything.

After some distance, as we took the turn from our lane, I gradually slowed down my bicycle so she could catch up with me. As a result, within a few seconds of riding, we were together. I responded like it was some coincidence, "Hi Supriya, how are you?"

She replied with the same bright smile, "Hi."

"So, do you leave daily at the same time?" I asked with a careless expression.

"No, I'm late today. Usually, I leave at 8.50 am," she replied.

We were both in our college uniform. Our conversation continued until we reached college.

While going to our respective classes, she told me that she would meet me at lunch. From the moment I entered my class, in one part of my mind, the countdown to lunch started.

We ate our lunch together. Eventually, our topics began to divert from college to our family. I was so engrossed that I hardly spoke to anyone in our college or colony.

Supriya lived with her parents and dadi. Her mom and dad worked in the same bank. So, most of the time, she spent her day with her dadi.

Over time, as our families' interaction became more frequent, our meetings extended from college to colony. However, Supriya's dadi did not like interacting with our family. For some reason, she hated our community (Jaats). She even instructed Supriya to maintain distance from our family.

In December, our semester exam started. The college closed for study leave for two weeks. Now with this, the major part of our meetings stopped. In winter, on sunny days, most families used to sit on their roofs to sunbathe. I could see Supriya studying on her roof.

Our roofs were around 100 metres apart, but the view was perfect. With this, I even started taking all my books there and did my studies on the roof terrace. It was a little surprising for my family, as I had never shown a preference to sit there. When our family members were not there, we used to play dumb charades for hours while acting out the names of different movies. While one person would act out the name of the film, the other would guess. We also used large sheets of paper to write down the names of the movies if the other person could not guess. Without talking, we spent some fabulous moments with each other. We even noted down the score for each other. We bet that whoever won would treat the other on the last day of our exam.

At this point, we started to call each other, but having a landline had consequences. When she called, if mom or dad picked up the phone, she hung up without saying a word. The sudden rise in the telephone bill made my parents suspicious that something was up. Somewhere, they know everything, but they did not bring it up.

Amusingly, whenever her dadi picked up the phone, I used to talk to her in a girl's voice. She never recognised my voice. Then one day, when I had just woken up, I called her. Her dadi answered the phone. I did not change the pitch of my voice but, as usual, introduced myself as Neha. That day, she scolded Supriya severely and gave her a warning that if it continued, she would tell her father.

Finally, our exams were over. She had won the game, so we decided to meet at the restaurant near our college. The restaurant was not a common meeting place then. We entered separately and sat at the corner table so that nobody would recognise us.

This was our first official date.

We talked about our family, college days, relatives and our likes and dislikes. I could feel her passion for her career. After lunch, we decided to go for a walk. The place was on the outskirts of the city, so we were not worried about somebody seeing us. We walked for an hour, talking about each other's lives. Then we decided to stop for ice cream.

The ice cream shop was completely empty. Inside, she told me to close my eyes. I could hear the sound of something being unwrapped. After a few seconds, as I opened my eyes, I saw her standing in front of me with a rose in her hand and a small gift-wrapped box in another.

She said, "I love you, dear. I don't know why and when, but I like you very much and request you to continue to live with me like this. The moment you came into my life, everything changed."

I was speechless. Over the last 2–3 months, we had become very open with each other because our conversations were unique. I had always wanted to propose to her, but I feared losing this precious friendship.

However, on that day, Supriya broke the veil between us. Everything felt like a fairy tale. I held her hand and kissed it with tears in my eyes. Then, she gave me the gift box containing a wristwatch, the most precious gift of my life. Considering the risk of damage, I have never worn that watch, but I always keep it close.

I told her that it was like some dream come true for me.

And thus, we entered a formal relationship. We used to meet at parks, movie theatres and, my favourite, our long bicycle rides to unknown parts of the city. By now, I was either with her or thinking about her all the time.

With time, our bond and understanding kept getting stronger.

A relationship with your senior makes you very well-known among your teachers and peers in colleges. By this time, even my mom and dad were pretty sure about our relationship. And Supriya's dadi also knew about us. Supriya never missed a chance to meet my mom—especially on Holi or Diwali, which we used to celebrate together.

My mom often tried to convince me that she was Punjabi and that dad would never accept our relationship. But dad never said anything directly to me. As time passed and our family realised that things had gone too far, everybody accepted our relationship.

As soon as Supriya completed her graduation, her mom and dad transferred to Bareilly. By this time, everything was well settled. Of course, there were some objections from my relatives, but surprisingly, dad always silently took my side and supported me. Seriously, I did not expect this from him. The rest were just formalities. We enjoyed a two-year long-distance relationship. With the permission of mom and dad, I visited Bareilly almost every month to meet Supriya. The moment I got a job after my graduation, we got married.

I had never been happier in my life.

Chapter 7.2

Once Upon a Time (Letter from Dad)

After my graduation, I started to work in a warehouse in Lucknow. The job was as an SAP data entry operator. Supriya was dynamic and intelligent since her college days. She planned to join the post-graduation programme at the same college before searching for a job. She had always wanted to do a job and all her future plans involved having a career.

From the first day of our relationship, I have respected her dreams. I even promised her that I would never impose my ideas on her. Even when I was convincing my family about our marriage, I used to mention her wish to do higher education and then take up a job. And my family never raised their eyebrows at this.

We were living a very peaceful and content life. The money that we earned was more than enough for our limited aspirations and expenses. What I like the most about that period is that we did not expect anything extraordinary from life. We were satisfied with whatever we had. Yes, at some point dad planned to own a house, but that dream never imposed any financial burden on us, as he planned on purchasing this house with his retirement funds. The daily routine was perfectly balanced between mom, dad, Supriya and my friends.

Everything was well-scheduled and adequately planned. Very soon, Supriya joined the MBA programme at the same college. The admission process was smooth as she was among the toppers in her batch.

After our marriage, Supriya fit in with our family quite quickly. I never felt any challenge on that count. In the morning, Supriya and mom prepared our breakfast and lunch. I left home at 9.30 am with dad on our Bajaj scooter. His office and my warehouse were about five kilometres away, so he used to drop me off first and then proceed towards his office. In the evening, we both reached home by 5.30 pm. At that time, staying extra hours at the office was not done. Nothing could be more simple, more stable and happier than that routine. Supriya also used to go to her college at ten am and return by three pm.

One day, Supriya wanted to watch a much-awaited movie in the theatre. So, after taking mom's and dad's permission, we planned to go to the movie the next Sunday. Since this theatre was near our home and we wanted to avoid any last-minute glitches, I purchased the ticket on Saturday. The next day, I took dad's scooter. We reached the theatre well before time.

In those days, there was no system of seat number allotment with the ticket. Hence, while entering the theatre, things were a bit disorganised. I observed some young guys deliberately falling on Supriya and trying to push her. In that kind of scenario, it was tough to say whether it was intentional or due to the crowd. So, I came in between, helped her and finally, we managed to enter. Just after the movie started, a group of young guys began to make rude comments. They were around 5–6 young men sitting right behind our seats. Initially, all these comments were generalised, but after the interval, maybe our silence made them braver. They started to comment specifically about Supriya. We ignored them and tried to concentrate on the movie. A few minutes later, they began to throw popcorn at us. When this happened, I turned around, pointed my finger at them and shouted that if they repeated this, they would have to face severe consequences. I remembered that these were the same people we had trouble with on our entry to the theatre. During all this, Supriya kept asking me to leave and return home. I was very irritated and wanted to teach them a lesson. When I observed the expression on her face change from sad to fearful, I took a deep breath, trying to calm myself down. But those silly guys continued passing cheap comments. Supriya held my hand and pulled me outside the theatre. I agreed with her since we did not want to spoil our much-awaited weekend. Supriya even tried to convince me that she did not like the movie and was feeling very hungry.

We came out of the theatre and decided to go to a popular restaurant near the theatre to have some snacks. We ordered her favourite chaat and lassi. Within a few minutes of ordering our food, I saw that the same guys from the theatre were rushing towards the restaurant. In a flash, they reached our table. Supriya was frightened and one of them said, "Come outside the restaurant. We want to talk to you!"

When this happened, Supriya held my hand and told me not to go anywhere. I got up from my chair and replied calmly, "See, guys, she is my wife and right now, I seriously don't want any trouble. If you…"

Before I could complete my sentence, he slapped me vigorously. It was so hard that the loud noise echoed throughout the restaurant. I fell to the table. A moment later, I balanced myself and dragged them away from the table, as I did not want Supriya to get hurt in between all of this. They were 6–7 men aged between 20–25 years. They sprinted towards me again, but this time I was prepared. I dashed forward, grabbed them and pushed one of them down. I slammed my knee into his face, but the next moment they came together, caught me from behind and started to punch my stomach so hard that I felt blood rushing into my mouth. I spit it out onto the floor. This continued for the next 10–15 minutes. They beat me up very badly and even tore my clothes. During all this, Supriya was screaming, asking people for help.

Finally, they left. She came and lifted me as I was lying on the floor. Blood flew down from my upper lip and the bottom side of my right eye. I groaned in pain as my back and, well, everything ached. While I struggled to stand, some people came over to help arrange a rickshaw. We went to a nearby hospital. At first, the doctor cleaned up all the blood. After further investigation, he told us that the cut on the upper lip was a little deep. So, he had to stitch it.

We came out of the hospital within an hour. Now I could walk with a little limp but without any support. As my clothes were not in a good condition, we went to the clothing store next to the hospital. We were planning to hide this entire incident from mom and dad (or at least as much as we could), but as we entered home, on seeing my face, instantly, mom figured out everything. By this time, my right eye had swollen up a little. Supriya narrated the incident. Dad wanted to file a police complaint, but mom and Supriya convinced him not to exaggerate the issue further. After a lengthy discussion and argument between mom and dad, he finally agreed.

Within an hour of this incident, everybody pretended to be normal. But my mind was seething. I wanted to meet those hooligans and beat them badly.

In the evening, I told Supriya I wanted to get some fresh air and came out of the house. I called all my friends and narrated the whole situation. We decided that we would find them immediately. As most of my friends lived in the same colony, within a few minutes, six of them arrived. Without wasting any time, we reached the place and started our search.

It was Sunday evening, so the market was a little crowded and it was falling dark. After 10–15 minutes of sweeping the area, I saw one of them sitting at a tea stall. When I pointed him out to my friends, they caught him and asked his name.

"Sanjay," he replied. My friends held his hands from behind and my first reaction was to slap him as hard as I could with my injured hand. But my slap made my friends lose their grip on Sanjay. With a quick jerk, he ran and crossed the main road.

While running, he did not notice a mini-truck coming down the road and it hit him. It was a head-on collision. We froze in our places. Everybody on the street started looking at us and many ran toward the accident location. Around 2–3 people caught my hand and I was not in a condition to resist. Some of them ran towards my friends, but they panicked and ran away.

They took me to the police station, around 200 metres away from that location. The officer-in-charge came out of his room and stood in front of me. Some of the police officers and the people who took me to the police station already knew Sanjay— they were using his name while narrating the incident. I tried to interrupt and correct their story, but nobody listened to me.

Eventually, he moved inside his room. Another policeman came and started to note down my personal information. As soon as he learned my father's name and home address, he sent another policeman to call my father. I was yelling and trying to describe the incident that happened in the morning, but none of them was interested. Meanwhile, the in-charge came out of his room and instructed the policeman standing next to me that if I continued to shout, he should beat me up.

Within half an hour, dad arrived at the police station. I was standing on the outer premises. As he walked toward me, I put my head down. Without even looking at me, he walked into the officer-in-charge's room. Coincidentally, in less than a minute, Sanjay's father also came in. He was well recognised and the police officers standing next to me addressed him respectfully. He looked wealthy and wore a heavy gold chain, a golden watch and shining white clothes from top to bottom. First, he stopped in front of me, crouched down to the level of my eyes while asking my name and finally went on to the officer's room.

One of the people who came with Sanjay's father walked up to me and whispered, "Sanjay's collar bone was fractured." he was staring at me intensely. After a few seconds of dangerous silence, he told me, "Sanjay is the son of the president of the Market Association, where you are standing right now. You have committed the biggest mistake of your life. Get ready to face the consequences now."

After some time, dad, Sanjay's father and the officer-in-charge came out of the room. My father walked out of the police station with a very displeased expression. I tried to call him, but he ignored me. Sanjay's father and the officer-in-charge were now standing in front of me. Sanjay's father asked the officer-in-charge to get an undertaking from me that if I repeated this kind of nonsense in the future, severe action would be taken against me. I tried to describe the morning's incident to him. He interrupted me and said that he already knew everything.

Sanjay's father finally pointed his finger at me and said, "Let me correct your misconception, dear. It's not about right or wrong here. I have given you a second chance because you are very young and belong to a good family. I didn't want to spoil your career at this stage of your life. Don't prove me wrong. Otherwise, the punishment will be very harsh and irretrievably damage your life."

Saying this, they moved out of the police station. But my father's expression while he was exiting the police station was running through my mind. I instantly ran towards home. It was already 8.30 pm and the house was around two kilometres away. I pressed the doorbell. Supriya opened the door and the moment she saw me, she started to weep and hugged me. I told her, "I am all right." Saying this, I wiped her tears. Lowering her voice, she said, "Sorry dear. I know all this happened because of me. I had been pressuring you to take me to the movie for so many days."

I just smiled looking into her eyes. "Believe me, it's not you. Please bring me a glass of water." As she turned towards the kitchen, I asked, "Where is Dad?" She responded by pointing toward dad's room. I tried to peep inside, but the door was almost shut. I reached for the door handle slowly, opened it slightly and saw dad sitting on one corner of the bed reading a book. I walked into the room and stood near him.

He did not notice, so I sat near his legs and said fumbling, "Dad..." He looked at me and went back to reading his book.

Again, I whispered, "Sorry, Dad!" This time, he did not react at all. I held his feet with both hands and repeated, "Sorry..."

His face was almost covered by the book. He replied very slowly but firmly, "You know, for the first time in my life, I had to plead with someone. In my entire life, I had never done this for myself. If I had done so, I would not have had to compromise on many things that could have eased and made my life more comfortable. Every time, I maintained my dignity. Today, I had to do that for you and I must say, you embarrassed me. There is hardly any difference between those guys and you."

I placed my head on his feet, tears flowing from my eyes. He pulled out his legs, leaned towards me and held me by the shoulders. I said, "Dad, something happened this morning. I wanted to take revenge for their deeds. I was not able to control my temper."

While I was saying all this, my voice started trembling. Dad stopped me and whispered in my ears, "Before taking any action, you must evaluate its impact on you and the people associated with you. You are a married man now. If you can't control your anger at this stage, then how will you manage your family in the future? Any spontaneous reaction will always bring disaster. If you don't care about the people waiting for you at home, sooner or later, you will become the reason for our fall. Just imagine if that boy, Sanjay, had died. You can't even imagine the tragedy that could befall us just because of your immaturity."

I had my head bent low and did not say anything. Meanwhile, I realised that mom and Supriya were standing next to me.

Mom put her hands on my shoulder and asked me to relax. Supriya gave me a glass of water. Dad stood up, put his hand around my shoulder and asked mom to make a special ginger tea for everyone. Smiling, mom and Supriya moved towards the kitchen and we moved towards the dining table. Both of us sat down, facing each other.

Dad said, "See, my motive is not to vex or offend you. You must understand the intensity of your mistake, learn a lesson from it and ensure that it is not repeated in the future. If this is implemented, there is no need to waste your time and effort carrying these bad memories. Just forget them. Consider them a bad dream."

I hugged him and my silence revealed my apology. When all of us were having tea, dad mentioned, "Now nobody will discuss this incident in the future; life is too long! We do not need to carry everything all the time."

After that day, we never discussed that incident. I avoided remembering that incident since I did not want to see Sanjay or any of his friends again. But it is impossible to predict what destiny has in store for you.

One day, while returning from our office, I saw Sanjay and his father in a car just behind us. This place was about 4–5 km from our house. Dad did not notice them. Our scooter was running very slow, approximately 30–40 kmph. I could see the cast on Sanjay's right hand extending up to his neck, where his fracture must have been. They were both looking at me while saying something to each other.

Their conversation ended in a burst of laughter while I was trying to avoid eye contact with them. Slowly, their speed started to increase and they were right next to us at one point. Till this time, dad had no idea about them.

The very next moment, they accelerated dangerously. Sanjay's dad stuck his head out his window and tried to spit his *paan* in front of our scooter. But there was a speed breaker in the way and we both had to reduce our speed. Sanjay's father could not control his reflexes and spat directly on dad's legs. Since dad was not aware of the presence of their car, this spitting shocked him. He lost his balance and our scooter fell on the road. But due to our low speed, dad balanced himself and supported me too. We hardly touched the ground. Without wasting a second, I ran towards their car, put my hand inside through the open window and removed the car keys while they were trying to escape. Without the keys, the car stopped soon after. I opened the door and dragged Sanjay's father out of the car, holding his collar with my right hand and a piece of stone that I'd picked up on the way in the other. Sanjay and my dad shouted simultaneously intending to stop me. Because of the anger, my head was spinning, my body shaking, my breathing rapid... At that moment, I wanted to kill the man. I cannot forget the horrified expression on Sanjay's father's face. We were both looking deep into each other's eyes. I seriously wanted to end it all, but somehow, I was able to pause for a few seconds.

Meanwhile, dad came and snatched the stone from my hand and slapped me hard across my face. I do not remember dad ever beating me before that, but yes, for this slap, I will always be thankful to him. Dad immediately pulled me away. I did not react, but my eyes were locked with Sanjay's dad. Something saved me that day.

What was this something?

- A man with nothing will resort to great extremes, while a man with everything to lose will try to hold on to the situation. A person with no prospect to look forward to in life, no family, no money, nowhere to go... Believe me, he is the most dangerous person ever to exist.

- A person with a happy family, home, plans for the future... This person will do anything to limit his losses. His decisions may contain shameful, insulting or illogical actions.

While returning home, I broke the silence between us and revealed the incident to dad. All these details about this incident shook dad and transformed his view. He stopped his scooter at one side of the road. After a long-drawn silence, he said, "Thankfully, you controlled your emotions at the last moment. Trust me, when I saw you holding Sanjay's dad's collar, I lost all hope and even started imagining the consequences. But you must learn one thing today. We live in a jungle here, with many dangerous and powerful animals around us. They don't think and react like human beings and live their life under their animalistic persona. They wouldn't want to lose their dominance in the community under any circumstance. They can take any action and go to any extent to save their image, status and power. If you are plotting to beat them up, in the area where they have leverage and power, which they exercise daily, then, believe me, they will soon slaughter you. But it doesn't mean they can't be defeated at all. The right approach at the right time and skill can do magic."

There is a difference between defeating and destroying someone, and your ultimate purpose will determine it.

My vision was blurred due to the tears. I asked, "Dad, how is all this to end?" Dad replied, "Now listen to me carefully. Just close your eyes and choose out of two options, which is more worthy and meaningful to you—is it your family's happiness and future or revenge on Sanjay? But keep one thing in mind, these two will not be possible at the same time. Both options have their rewards and punishments. So, the decision is yours. If I impose anything on you, it will be useless."

I took a deep breath, tried to calm myself down and wiped the tears off my face in the next few minutes. I took my handkerchief from my pocket, soaked it in water from a nearby tap and started to clean the *paan* stain from dad's trousers. Dad was standing quietly and steadily while I cleaned. I replied, "Dad, nothing in this world is more important than my family. I don't even have to consider the alternatives." On hearing this, dad pulled me up holding my shoulder. He turned his scooter, started it and asked me to sit behind him.

After driving for 10–15 minutes, taking a few twisting bylanes, he stopped his scooter in front of a vast entrance gate. It looked like the entrance of a huge bungalow.

"Whose place is this, Dad and why are we here?" I asked while getting off the scooter.

Dad replied while parking the scooter on the main stand, "It's Sanjay's house."

Now, this was unexpected. "Dad...? Why are we here now? Sometimes I don't understand you."

"We came here so that you will make up with Sanjay and his father. And you have the entire responsibility of handling this situation," Dad said while knocking on the door.

"But Dad, what if he becomes aggressive and doesn't accept my apology? Are you sure about this?" I kept arguing and asking, wishing that he would stop and we could go back home.

Meanwhile, the door opened and a person stepped out. Before he could ask anything, dad said, "We're here to see Sanjay's father."

The man at the door turned and motioned us to come inside and follow him. Inside the premises, everything was much larger than it seemed from the outside. There was a huge grass lawn inside, surrounded by dense trees. At the centre of the garden was a group of 20–25 people standing in a circle. We were going directly towards them. As we reached closer to them, there was absolute silence. The men separated and turned towards us. Sanjay sat on the sofa at the centre of this group with his father.

He stared at me and started to get on the offensive, but his father held him back. Our presence was a shock to him too. Before they could react, I came face-to-face with Sanjay's father, went down on my knees and joining my hands said, "We came here to apologise. I am sorry for my behaviour today. Everything that happened today was in the heat of the moment. Believe me, it wasn't planned or intentional at all."

Dad was standing just behind me. Watching him so helpless was the most painful part of the ordeal for me.

After listening, I could see Sanjay's father's expression change as he got a dose of power and lost pride in front of all his people.

Sanjay was not looking satisfied, I again made eye contact with him and said, "See, Sanjay, I know that in the theatre, you were just part of those guys, being led by the other guys. I am sure it could have all been avoided. I am sorry for my actions and promise you that nothing of this sort will ever happen again."

Sanjay's father replied, "Son, I am delighted to see you here, admitting your mistake. You have your whole life in front of you.

Look at your father. See how much of a gentleman he is. You can't even imagine how quickly I can ruin your life, God knows. By coming here, you have saved yourself and your family from a dangerous storm."

During this episode, I kept my head bowed and replied in the most submissive way, as expected by Sanjay and his father, without thinking about it too much.

With this, we returned home. Believe me, from the moment we returned after our conversation till this second, we never discussed or shared that incident with anyone. Even mom and Supriya have no idea about this.

It was difficult to agree when dad told me to apologise to Sanjay and his father. Indeed, as a youngster with an ego and having been fairly humiliated, I felt it was unforgivable. This story occupied a small portion of my heart for the rest of my life. The lesson I learned was incredible. Dad's understanding of Sanjay's father and my feelings were right. The place where this whole incident happened used to fall under the area where Sanjay's father was the president. Everybody knew him there and since I grabbed his collar in front of everyone, dad knew he would surely take intense retaliatory action. This was the only way in which things could have settled down. He knew what he was doing all the time, so he managed to change the outcome.

You need to adopt the right approach to solve any problem. Sometimes, situations could change into tragedies if appropriate action is not taken at the right time.

Most importantly, to understand everything, I had to calm my head, but dad planned and executed this when the situation was at its peak. He indeed won my heart with his strategic manoeuvring.

Chapter 7.3

The Devil (Letter from Dad)

After completing her post-graduation, Supriya learned many software tools and languages apart from her regular college course. From the beginning, she was very passionate about learning new things. She had a habit of reading various computer magazines and updating herself about upcoming technology. In the initial days of our marriage, she did not even know about cooking essential dishes and other routine housework. But with the support of mom, very soon, she could handle the majority of kitchen work alone, if needed.

Before leaving for college, she used to prepare breakfast and pack our tiffin. She also prepared dinner in the evening. Even with all these responsibilities, she managed to spare time that she utilised for her studies. Like her graduation, she completed her post-graduation with good grades and soon got a job in one of the most prestigious companies in Lucknow. At that time, only two multinational companies had their branches in Lucknow and because of her dedication, your mom got a job in one of them. As this company had established their branches just six months ago, most of their staff was new, except for their boss, Rahul sir, who had recently transferred from their Delhi office. There was a total of fifteen employees and there were only two females, including Supriya.

Supriya was very excited about this job. It was like a dream come true for her. She told me a lot of times how lucky she was that even after her marriage, she had the opportunity to study and then land a job since, at that time and in that location, girls getting a job was not a thing that was approved by relatives or neighbours.

Actually, they had their reasoning behind this narrow thinking. Then, the city atmosphere was unfavourable because of widespread rape, chain snatching and robbery incidents. You could not imagine any woman being alone on the streets after seven in the evening.

After she got her job, I purchased a brand-new Rajdoot. At that time, it was considered a very royal vehicle to own. This was mainly because I had to drop off and pick up Supriya from her office daily. Her office timings were from 10:00 am to 5:30 pm. If ever she was running late, then I used to wait for her outside her office.

Almost daily, during dinner, she told us everything about her office and her routine. We knew her immense love and dedication to her work. One night, when we were about to sleep, she said, "I want to tell you something." After two years of marriage, it was pretty clear to me that this was something serious that she wanted to share, as her voice was fumbling and heavy. I replied, "Yes, dear, please share with me."

She responded, "For the last 2–3 days, I've wanted to discuss something with you, but I can't figure out how. I'm not even sure about its intensity and reality. All this could be my imagination. But I don't want you to overreact to this."

"Oh dear, I know you very well now, don't worry," I replied.

She continued, "As you know, our office has a very joyful environment. We laugh and tease each other most of the time. But for the last few days, I've observed that my boss, Rahul sir, is stretching this teasing a bit more than usual. Overall, he is a very kind and helpful person. He has guided me and everyone in the office on this project. He is always ready to help. But in the last few days, some of the incidents happening in the office are making me uncomfortable. Like today, while I was sitting at my desk, he explained some project-related things. Most of the time, he keeps his hands on my shoulder, or while greeting me in the morning, he holds my hands for a moment too long. There are many more minor incidents to which I cannot decide how to react. This is making me uncomfortable. I am not sure about them too. Sometimes, I really cannot figure out if I should consider all these incidents as crossing a line. Rahul sir behaves this way with Shila, the other female colleague in my office. However, she is absolutely comfortable with all this. I tried to discuss this with her, but she told me that since I started my professional journey recently, all these things could look abnormal or new to me. Apparently, all these are very common in the corporate world. To exist here, I have to adapt to them. Her words shocked me a little. Shila also said that the ultimate truth is that he is our boss who helps us most of the time and that these silly little things should not be considered worth bothering about."

Now Supriya had transferred all of her doubts and tension into my mind. She was right—the situation was not that straightforward. It was very difficult for me to classify them as either white or black. I told her, "Often, we start to look at things from other people's points of view. I suggest you think about every situation at a broad level—no need to consider small situations with a negative point of view. Or develop a habit of doubting everyone from every angle. Because if you do so, everything in this world will turn out adverse to you. But never hesitate to speak about it. Because if there is even a 1% chance that the other person's intention is not good, your silence also sends a message. It's better to react at the correct time, with a positive attitude and in a calm manner. For example, if he stares at you often, then don't look away but stare back till he backs off, or if he stands too close to you in the lift or chair, then turn around and look him in the eye and say, 'Sorry sir, but there is enough space around, and I am sure you don't realise it, but you are making me uncomfortable. Do you mind standing back a little? Thank you.'"

It seems Supriya got my message. I promised her that she could discuss any doubt and that she should never feel alone. I would always stand with her and support her.

The next day, as she came out of her office building, she looked delighted. I was standing on the road in front of her building and she told me to stop at the nearby park as she wanted to share something that happened in her office that day. She said, "I am giving you a treat today." We went to the nearby park and sat on the bench there. Immediately, she went to the canteen and purchased two ice creams.

Handing me a cone, she started, "You know, today afternoon, as we were having lunch in the office, all of us were sitting at a circular table—Rahul sir, Shila and the other two team members. I observed twice that somebody hit on my legs below the table. I was unsure if it was an accident or if someone was intentionally doing this. But in the form of a joke, I explained to everyone and gave a clear message that I did not like this. I also pulled my chair a little backward. You know, after this, Shila figured out the situation and looked at me with surprise. The other team members did not take much notice of my words, but the expression on Rahul sir's face was remarkable. It showed tension and fear, but he tried to cover it with a smile. Later he came to my desk many times, but not even once did he keep his hand on my shoulder or do anything else that made me uncomfortable. Your idea worked. Thank you, my hero."

The next day, while we were returning from Supriya's office, she told me, "Next Monday, my company wants me to visit Delhi. They told me today and even booked my train ticket for the same. But I made it very clear to them that I couldn't commit without discussing it with my family."

I replied with enthusiasm, "But what is the purpose of this visit?"

She replied, "A new project is about to start in our branch. The company wanted to hand over this project to me as a team leader at our head office in Delhi."

"You are going alone?" I asked.

"No, Rahul sir is also coming with me. We must present in front of our entire team there."

"Wow, dear, this is good news. I don't know why you are so stressed. Don't worry about mom and dad. We will convince them. At this time, you need to concentrate on preparing for your presentation," I said.

During dinner, she told them about being appreciated by her team leader for completing the project. She also informed them about her visit to Delhi. Mom was a little hesitant and tense about her travelling alone. Mom even told me to take leave and travel with Supriya.

I told her, "Don't bother, Mom, it will be a single-day journey. Anyway, I will not get leave from my office on such short notice."

Mom asked, "So, what will be the timing of the train?"

Supriya replied, "At 6:30 am, the train departs from Lucknow station and returns around 11:00 pm."

I intervened, "Don't worry, I will be there to drop you off and pick you up."

Dad said, "I am impressed with your commitment to your work. Keep going."

Supriya was thrilled. She immediately touched mom and dad's feet. She was very excited about her presentation. She rehearsed it so many times in front of mom and me that even we memorised half of it.

On Monday, we reached the railway station at 5:30 am. Rahul sir was already there at the main entrance of the railway station, waiting for us. He had a great personality and was aged between 45–50 years. Supriya introduced us.

"The train is already at the platform. Since this is the starting station, it's better if we settle down," I said.

Then at 6:00, the train started and I said goodbye as the train began to move. Supriya reminded me to reach precisely at 11:00 pm to pick her up at night.

I replied, "Okay, don't worry about that. Just concentrate on your presentation and all the very best."

At night, I reached the railway station at 10:45 pm and confirmed at the inquiry counter that the train was well on time and would arrive within ten minutes. Finally, the train arrived. I was already standing in front of her compartment. When the train stopped, I boarded the train and moved towards their reserved seat number. When I reached there, I was shocked, as Supriya was not there. Two railway policemen were sitting at the window seat, which was supposed to be Supriya's seat. In between them, Rahul sir was sitting in handcuffs. I was shocked and asked Rahul sir, "What happened here? Where is Supriya?"

One of the policemen answered in a sleepy voice, "Who are you?"

"Her husband," I replied.

"Go to seat number 54," he replied.

"Is she alright?" I asked him, tense.

"She is absolutely okay. Just go there," the policeman replied.

I ran towards the seat number. Supriya was sitting in the window seat. When she saw me, she immediately stood up from her seat, hugged me and started crying like a small child.

I drew back and asked her while staring into her eyes, "What happened, dear? Tell me."

She quickly picked up her bag and said, "I will tell you everything, but first, let's get off this train."

We quickly got off the train and then started to move out of the railway station without exchanging a single word. She was running and I followed her, thinking about millions of possibilities. As we came outside the railway station, we sat on a bench outside, beside a tea stall.

I held her hand and said, "Now tell me what happened. Why were you sitting on a different seat? Why did the police handcuff Rahul sir? What is the matter?"

She replied, "When our presentation got over, we rushed back to the railway station. It was only 2.30 pm and we still had two hours until the train was scheduled to come. The station was hardly fifteen minutes from our head office. Rahul sir asked me to have some food saying that the food at the railway station had been terrible in the morning. We found a restaurant near the station and I ordered some light snacks with tea. But surprisingly, he ordered some hard drinks for himself. Initially, I rebuked him and said, 'Sir, you are not supposed to have drinks right now.' But he replied, 'I am sorry dear, I have to drink some as I am a habitual drinker and very stressed at this moment. I don't feel relaxed without this.' He did not even eat any of the food he ordered and continued to drink. After I finished my meal, we moved towards the railway station. He was completely drunk while we sat in the car, he tried to hold my hands many times, but when I called him out, he apologised and said it had happened by mistake. Finally, we boarded the train. Our seats were opposite each other, so we sat facing each other. Because of his behaviour, I was terrified and wanted to reach Lucknow as soon as possible. Since I was utterly exhausted, within an hour, my eyes started to shut. The train was not crowded. Three seats were vacant in our section. But after some time, I felt a slight uneasiness. It was like maybe something was touching my legs and shoulder. Initially, I thought it could be someone's bag, but when I opened my eyes, I was shocked and screamed my lungs out. Rahul sir was sitting next to me. His face was close to mine and his hand was on my thigh. I stood up and ran towards the passage screaming. My behaviour caught the attention of the other passengers. One old lady sitting on the side berth requested me to calm down and she offered me her seat. I told her everything. When she heard of the incident, she woke up her son sleeping on the upper berth and gathered the other passengers. Some of the passengers called the police officers already inside the train. They beat Rahul sir severely, but he was hardly in his senses. Then, they handcuffed him. They asked me to get off at the next station for further proceedings against him, but I refused and asked them to take action at the Lucknow station. I can't tell you how I am feeling right now, but you promised me that you would not do anything violent and stupid. Believe me, I can't take any more stress at this moment. We will file an FIR and follow other police procedures."

I put my hand on her head, gave her a water bottle and tried to calm her down. Then, without wasting any time, we reached home, called mom and dad, explained the whole situation to them and proceeded to the railway station for further police procedures.

When we entered the railway police station, Rahul sir was sitting on the side bench. We entered the officer-in-charge's room. He noted down Supriya's complete statement. Supriya was a bit hesitant to elaborate on the details of the incident, so dad moved outside. With this, the police officers filed an FIR. While dad was outside, I took their officer-in-charge to one corner of the room and secretly bribed him to prepare the most robust charge sheet against Rahul. "This rascal must be screwed as hard as possible."

After some other formalities, we came out of the police station. Dad was waiting for us outside. When he saw Supriya coming out of the police station looking depressed, he hugged her and for the first time in my life, I saw tears in his eyes. He said, "Don't worry, we are always with you."

Dad seemed very anxious at that moment. We returned home. Everyone was trying their best to calm Supriya down. Mom made her favourite onion paratha. It was 1.30 am and finally, another hectic day ended.

In the morning, Supriya got ready as she did routinely. We were surprised to see her, but nobody intervened. On the way to her office, I told her, "If you want, you can take some days off and relax at home." She replied with determination that she needed to attend the office that day. She asked me to wait when we reached her office since she would be back in 15–20 minutes. Without any question, I agreed and she hurried to her office.

After thirty minutes, she returned and sat behind the bike without saying anything to me. She looked a little worried but tried to hide her stress. I started the bike and took her to the park's main entrance. We entered the park and sat on our usual bench.

Looking down, I held her hand and asked her, "What happened?"

"I have given my resignation. I can't work in this company any longer. You know, yesterday in Delhi, our presentation was fabulous and everybody appreciated my work. But this place is full of morons, thinking from their dirty and cheap minds. They view women in a derogatory manner and the most shocking thing is that their education has failed to enlighten their minds." With this, Supriya placed her head on my shoulder and we remained quiet for the next few minutes.

"I even sent one mail to our VP and MD, informing them about this incident and attached a copy of the FIR with my complaint. I seriously want Rahul to be thrown out of this company," Supriya said with an expression of frustration.

"Supriya, even I find myself helpless in this scenario. One part of my mind says to forget everything and destroy them so that no trace of their existence remains, but another part reminds me of my family and what you had to go through," I said.

"Anyway, forget all this. I will take an off today and take you to the riverfront," I said while coming out of the park, holding her hand. Before marriage, we used to go there very frequently.

After 4–5 days, a 40–45-year-old person visited our home at two pm in the afternoon. He was dressed formally and looked decent. As it was a Saturday, all of us were home. When I opened the door, he greeted me and said, "My name is Surya Prakash, I am from the head office of Supriya's company and I wanted to meet her regarding the incident." I called Supriya. When she saw the man, she recognised him and introduced him as the HR Head of her company. We were sitting in our drawing room. The guy apologised on behalf of the company for the train incident and showed us the letter of dismissal of Rahul Singh.

"This guy will not get any job in any of our companies for the rest of his life," he said. Subsequently, he handed over a letter of appointment, requesting Supriya to join their company again. But Supriya refused point blank. Even after repeated requests from him, Supriya did not accept the letter. He placed the letter on the table and said, "Ma'am, we respect your decision, but if you wish to join our company, not only in Lucknow but anywhere in India, it will be our pleasure."

With this, he left. But this incident planted a seed in my brain. *Why couldn't we move to some other city and settle there?*

A city where Supriya could join her job without any feeling of fear, where goons did not rule the city, where people could live without any doubt about their security and focus on the single agenda of growth, where men did not x-ray each and every woman around them, where we could provide our future children with a perfect platform to learn and experience the changing world.

One of my friends called Ajay lived in Bombay. He finished his graduation with me and then did his MBA from Bombay University. Ajay moved to Bombay and settled there with his family. I called him and told him about my plan. After getting feedback about the city from Ajay, I thought that even if the city was half as good as he described, it was worth discussing this idea with Supriya and dad.

I talked with Supriya and dad during dinner time. They were very supportive of my idea. Dad suggested, "You can do one thing, take leave and visit Bombay. Check the possibility of getting a job there. It is better to make a decision after having some personal experience."

Chapter 7.4

The Separation from Roots
(Letter from Dad)

This incident was my turning point. Sometimes, you arrive at a juncture in your life where you have to choose your future direction. These directions would lead you to unpredictable destinations. Before making a decision, you must consider the people who will be impacted by your choice. On the one hand, I had my parents with their lovely home full of beautiful memories and on the other hand, the future where I could see my and Supriya's professional careers grow, more financial stability and better opportunities for my future children.

That day, I decided I would not settle in Lucknow. This was not the place where I wanted my children to grow up. And after all this, the one thing that was very obvious to me was that if I stayed here any longer, sooner or later, I would lose my patience and end up in a tragic situation.

Very honestly, in the final moments of both incidents, I received some blessings in my life. They guided me and my decisions were influenced by my family. At that point in time, the best solution according to me was to run away from the mess.

Chapter 7.5

The Root Cause

Some rules are directly imposed by society and shape our minds. Surprisingly, our mind starts to adapt to these rules without even notifying us. Since our birth, this learning leaves a profound impact on us. It begins to act as a reference point for all our activities.

For example, all of us are pre-programmed to assume that **The majority is always right**, ethically or factually, even if they are not. They are ultimately declared the winners on social and emotional levels.

The win itself comes with the 'everything's right' tag.

From the childhood stories we hear, the books we read, to the movies we see, everything moulds our minds strongly: The good guys always win. The losing side is always defined as the story's evil or dark side. But in real life, things can never be black or white. Everything rides on different combinations of both, forming a different shade every time. In between these shades, winning or losing depends upon our perspective.

As we can see, the above two perceptions are complementary to each other and form a winning package.

We often conclude that the various reasons listed below are responsible for the chaos, which is the fundamental reason for any migration.

- Lack of Education

- Poverty

- Political Power or Social System

We tend to choose an easy target. It is always easy to place the blame on the system and politicians. Surprisingly, sometimes we blame God too!

Most of the time, when this migration issue is discussed on some broad platform, people and political parties promote them from their point of view. People from the other side have their own understanding of this situation.

- How are these migrants responsible for any mismanagement?

- How unfortunate, undisciplined or underdeveloped are these migrants?

- How have they ruined their home and now come here to do the same in our place?

Meanwhile, people in the lower rungs always consider people on the higher rungs of society as heartless and cruel.

I do not defend or attack the above questions because they could be justified too, to some extent. But have you ever heard of any solution from anywhere?

Whom are we waiting for?

What do you think, whose responsibility is it to react first?

Remember, these are the two sections of our society. The lower section always moves toward a higher one. This movement of people from the lower section towards the higher rungs of society can be defined as migration. As a result of this movement, when they come in contact with each other, it causes a collision. Directly or indirectly, all of us contribute to forming these two sections of society, so it is everyone's responsibility. Because no matter how successful we become, or have the best lifestyle or social status, a successful person of any community/region/caste can achieve not more than the average value of everyone (combining the higher and lower rungs of people).

It means some or the other way, all those worthless/underdeveloped/poor people will appear to us as a disturbance in our luxury. We cannot just separate them from being part of society by building a wall or using security forces between us and them. When they see us enjoying all those incredible, luxurious things, while they are struggling to manage necessities, they will use unethical ways to grab the same. That is the law. Everything in this world has the natural tendency to balance itself and nobody can alter that.

The above scenario can be explained by taking the simple experience of traffic and road accidents. We want to be safe on the road, reduce the probability of an accident and save time by reducing traffic jams. What do we have to do? We can go to some of the best driving institutes, fine tune our driving skills and then return to the road. After our actions, how much will the possibility of us having an accident on the road reduce?

Will driving better help us reduce traffic jams on the road?

Believe me, with our individual effort, there will be negligible improvement in the situation. Road accidents and traffic jams do not depend on our driving skills alone! Even with perfect driving, there is a significant risk of being involved in an accident if some unskilled driver is driving on the same road.

Now, if you ask me, is the unskilled driver stupid?

I will say yes!

Must he/she be punished? I will reply yes!

Because of his/her stupidity, he/she risks everybody's life on the road. So, should he/she be hanged? Or punished severely?

Now, my voice may fumble a little, but... maybe yes.

In the end, the question remains, will it reduce our probability of being involved in an accident if we do so?

Since the number of unskilled drivers is a million times more than the number of skilled ones, we cannot kill or punish them all. Do not forget that these incompetent people are in the majority.

So, what can be done now?

We must put in our best effort to provide driving training to all. And now we cannot say it is not our responsibility because the better they drive, the lesser our chances of getting into an accident on the road.

What is going wrong in these underdeveloped parts of the same country? How could a distance of 400–500 km change people and their thinking?

Comparing crime figures, rape, robbery, chain snatching and the million other types of fraud between two regions will give us a clear idea about the direction of migration between them.

Most of the time, the primary factor that leads to this failure to maintain a social balance is hidden in a single word: Lie. The majority of our society will never be able to catch up with the pace of this continuously changing world. The backward group of people may look different, but from their point of view, our so-called developed or modern lifestyle is not justified when compared to their old one.

They are the masters of their competencies since they still think modernisation and development are a piece of shit (whatever may be the reason for this thinking) and because they are present in large numbers. For them, every action is self-justified and approved.

Because our secret is based on our lies. Now, what does this lie mean?

If the things we are doing, saying and even thinking about are an effect of the thoughts and desires of others and not our own, it is in fact a lie. We may temporarily change its meaning by force or majority, but it will always remain a lie. A lie is practically what defines us. When the truth offends us, we close our eyes and lie until we cannot remember that it exists or is even practically possible. Still, in reality, it can never be eliminated. No matter if the majority of people accept a lie, the truth cannot be destroyed; it will always be present. Whenever people come face-to-face with it, they feel inadequate, get violent, try to destroy it and ultimately make a mess of things. Every lie we support will be a factor in long or short-term destruction.

Right after our birth, we are given the training to accept these lies and this falsity is continuously praised and imposed by society. This teaching of a myth includes countless tags with associated protocols that have to be followed blindly by all of us. All these are socially approved. If someone fails to follow these protocols, society will disown them, laugh at them, call them a symbol of failure and lower their status in the community.

But what are these tags and protocols?

These tags are the guidelines to behave and live among us. Divided into countless categories based on religion, community, caste, physical appearance, region, where a particular person lives, the social status of his/her family, education and much more. A set of rules defines how we should live, react, eat, feel or express ourselves in society.

This can be explained by the simple example of road rage. What factors make people hyper or short-tempered?

This is because their teachings are based on lies. After practising these lies for so long, the lies become their essence. Now, it is their responsibility to protect these tags blindly. For them, it is not acceptable that people dominate them; nobody can insult them. Since they belong to a particular class/community/religion/caste/social status and have unique protocols, it is their responsibility to protect them. It is not their fault since society has trained them in this manner. Their elders have been transferring these teachings from one generation to another.

Just look around us. Everybody is lying and we know that. But the major problem is that we are not interested in the truth based on fact; instead, we are more interested in the lies that are not converted into a reality based on being socially accepted or are instantly convenient to us.

Chapter 7.6

Towards the Horizon (Letter from Dad)

Since I spoke to Ajay, I had been in continuous touch with him. When we were in college, we were on the same wavelength. Ajay also wanted me to shift to Bombay so his family would have some company. Most of the time, he used to update me about upcoming openings. I even visited Bombay twice for job interviews but failed on both occasions. At that time, I was enthusiastic about getting a job and settling in Bombay. I kept discussing with Ajay about the lifestyle there and narrated everything to mom, dad and Supriya when I got back home.

Supriya was pretty fascinated by the city and was excited to shift there. She had even sent an inquiry to the previous company's HR, referring to the letter Mr Surya Prakash had given her. It had been around 3.5 years since she had left that company. Fortunately, she received an acknowledgement from their HR team. They said they did not have any vacancy then but promised to contact her shortly as there would be an opening in their Bombay office.

Mom and dad were okay with it too, but I knew that our enthusiasm for Bombay was hurting them internally and it was subtly visible. Long ago, when dad was posted in Kanpur and I was in the final year of my graduation, mom lived with me in Lucknow. There was hardly any weekend when dad did not come to meet us. Dad once told me that separation from us would be painful for them, but I should take it as a sacrifice for a better future for my family. Then after a long pause, he said, "This is what this new generation describes as growth."

I replied, "Don't worry, Dad, one day I will return and we will live the same life again, or Dad, even both of you can plan to shift there." Dad did not answer but just pretended to smile and hugged me.

It took me a lot of time to understand dad's fake smile. I knew that mom and dad did not agree or had some doubts about some of my decisions, but they did not stop us. I do not know whether they ever wanted to stop us from exploring this new world or did not want to force their old ways on us.

Meanwhile, Ajay suggested that I should complete a software course related to the development of SAP. It was a three-month course and its certification exam was to be held in Delhi. Luckily, from that year, preparation classes were available in Lucknow itself. I took admission and completed all my classes with my commitment, and assistance from Supriya since this was Supriya's area of interest. We often divided my subjects. She took my classes and cleared most of my doubts. Finally, quite comfortably, I succeeded in getting the certification. Within a month of getting my certification, Ajay notified me that there was one vacancy in his office created solely for the SAP profile. And finally, with Ajay's help and my certification, I made it to Bombay. It took almost three years of struggle to land this job.

Meantime, you came into this world. After celebrating your first birthday, with many aspirations and ignoring the uneasy sensation of moving away from our place, we moved to Bombay.

The salary I was offered at my new job was almost twice what I was receiving in Lucknow. But as we hurriedly shifted to Bombay, I understood that only the amount of my salary had doubled. The overall value reduced drastically when compared to Lucknow. I literally mean very drastically. Very soon, most of our dreams with which we came were forgotten in the rush for survival.

But all our various experiences had definitely trained both of us a lot. Moving away from our parents and home affected me immensely, most of it in ways that moulded me into a responsible grown-up. Initially, it was difficult, but changes are always tricky. I learned to let go of things and be on my own. We learned to cook, wash clothes and manage our money independently. Living our life without expectations from anyone around us, we started developing social relationships. We learned to groom ourselves physically and emotionally. We learned to create our own beliefs and passions. Most of all, we learned to survive.

It could be any situation or circumstance. You realise that you are on your own and you have to struggle to come out of it while adjusting or adapting, which is a beautiful life lesson...

Out of my ₹1400 salary in Lucknow, I could purchase most of the household groceries. Everything used to cost me approximately ₹800. With this being the expenditure for the whole month, I lived in a misconception. How well was I managing our house there?

But dad never burdened me with the other details. The role of a beam in a building can only be understood when it breaks. Otherwise, our whole life, on seeing the beauty of the walls, we live in the misconception that it is the walls that hold up the building and praise the walls.

While we were moving here, dad had given some backup money to Supriya in addition to our small savings. After settling down, our savings started to dwindle. But all this management made for a delightful stress between Supriya and me. We kept planning to buy a new home and utilities and accordingly started keeping aside small amounts for the next month. Your sickness or some surprise last-minute expenses often ruined everything for the rest of the month, but we started the saving cycle again. If our salaries were delayed by even 2–3 days, we had to rely on the backup amount given by dad. That phase was unique and we enjoyed it.

As time passed, things started to settle down. In this new city, Ajay's family was our only point of contact. So, we frequently visited each other's houses and spent weekends together. Our apartments were also in the same building. The new city came with its challenges and struggles. Having entirely different cultures, festivals, gods, languages, food habits and circumstances created several complications. Initially, all these challenges were exciting and were adventures to get through.

Yes, many things managed to amaze me out here, continuously justifying my decision to shift here since I had never assumed they could even exist. During my initial days, I was working shifts. During my evening shift, I used to reach home by 12.30 am. A company bus used to drop me near Kalyan local station and it was an entirely different world to me. Women and girls of all ages would return alone from their offices without any sign of fear or stress on their faces.

On top of that, after 11.30 pm, on another side of the road, sex workers used to wait for their customers to pick them up. This attracted some rascally crowds from nearby places; most of them would be drunk and could hardly walk. Although the above two incidents would happen simultaneously on two different sides of the road, the thing that disturbed me the most was that none of them appeared to be in conflict. The drunkards were not even looking at the women returning from their offices (I do not know what makes women/girls returning from their offices so confident that even in this scenario, they still feel safe, without the presence of any policemen nearby!), nor were the men returning from their offices reacting to the sex workers. Many times, I used to stop and observe this to find hidden aspects. But I could not find any and this scenario surprised me every time. It was hard to imagine any of these two things existing in Lucknow at that time. People would have killed each other for any minor issue.

After getting down from my shift vehicle, I had to travel down two stations on the local train to reach home. In the morning and evening, there were huge crowds on the trains, which meant that you could not get in or out of the train without elbowing people like they were inanimate obstacles, but I never saw any violence here. People have a natural tendency to make queues here. Until then, I had never seen people making queues without the police or any forceful external action. Traffic on the road during peak hours was incredible; roads were full of cars, buses and two-wheelers, and people were crossing roads everywhere, but I hardly saw any road rage cases. I was sure there was not much difference in people's driving skills here compared to Lucknow. When relating the stress level induced by the two cities, then considering people's average travel time, their hectic schedule, the workload in their offices, efforts to manage their kids and a million other factors, nobody could beat this place. Thousands of minor incidents like this forced me to think; what drove people here to be more disciplined and accountable than Lucknow?

But I was very sure that education and money were not the primary factors in controlling the social behaviour of people here. Yes, the people here did not behave perfectly, but the way they behaved was unquestionably superior to that of people in Lucknow.

Within six months of my joining here, Supriya got a reply from her former office for an interview and as she had been preparing for it for the last four years, she qualified pretty easily. It further helped us to stabilise our financial situation. When Supriya and I went to our offices for the first few days, Ajay's wife took care of you in her house. But after a few days, we decided to admit you to a playschool that was very close to Supriya's office and she started to handle both her job and you very well. And to chase our dreams, we became more involved in our professional life.

During our initial days, we were living in our self-created cocoon. Bombay meant our family, Ajay's family and our offices. So, external factors did not affect us much. Additionally, we had a long to-do list to be accomplished for our family and its future. We could not afford to distract ourselves.

While chasing our to-do list, somewhere, unwillingly, the personal touch between Supriya and me started to disappear. There were no significant issues between us. But we hardly sat together and never discussed anything about ourselves or each other's feelings like before. Most of the time, we talked about our financial outlines, plans to buy a new house, education plans for you, purchase of a new car and various other material things. With all this, we soon developed a new dimension in our personal and professional relationships. We often shared our office incidents, including topics related to our ongoing projects, and the pressure of completing tasks.

At that point in time, we did not realise that this unbalancing had started to happen in our lives. Considering that after so much waiting, Supriya finally had an opportunity to build her career, she liked everything about her job. However, she did not want to compromise on her family for her professional aspirations. Every day, she visited the playschool at least 3–4 times to meet you. She kept running between her office and your playschool.

It was not easy for me to survive in this new profile as well. All the tasks were big hurdles for me. I had to visit different sites, 3–4 days a month and was usually late, reaching home after nine pm.

This new city mothered us and coated us with its colour and culture. It really transformed us into being 'modern' and 'professional' in the true meaning of the words.

The Human Thought Process: Where it all started

Hunger. Science defines it as a feeling of discomfort or weakness caused by a lack of food, coupled with the desire to eat.

But within itself, it holds millions of vibrant flavours and nobody can ever imagine its true flavour until they experience it. Hence, its true meaning can be described thus:

Initially, it produces a sense of uneasiness in the body. Drinking water works as some relief and acts as a filler for the stomach. After a few hours, uneasiness starts to give way to a burning sensation. Annoying feelings start to fly all around you. Your mind instructs you to stop everything and intake food on top priority. By this time, the stomach understands the trick behind the water and denies any kind of relief from it. Within a few more hours, weakness can be felt in parts of your body, resulting in absolute heaviness. Your awareness of your atmosphere starts to diminish. Soon after, your eyelashes refuse to stay up. Your vision darkens with every passing second. The tongue starts to skip words. The stomach begins to feel like it is filled with acid and a deep sensation of decaying body parts starts to sweep through your body. You neither have the energy to shout nor to cry at the pain that pervades every part.

Our thoughts are always driven by our desires. They always change and hold a direct connection with the state of our stomach. An empty stomach does not understand any logic or rules of this world. Things like relationships or thoughtful instructions from society are out of its understanding. The most important thing it requires is food to kill its hunger. In this state, it readily accepts or agrees to play any role in this world without understanding the consequences.

A satisfied stomach always looks for security since it recently tasted the pain of being empty. So, it does not want to repeat this at any cost. At this point, its state of mind is even more submissive to this requirement. Once somebody has experienced hunger, this becomes the biggest fear for the rest of his/her life. Hence, to stave off hunger, one would take any action to any extent to prevent it in the future.

The moment they sense security, people take a little break and start to observe other people around them. They try to understand the events happening around them. But things have not been settled for a long time, as they have now discovered new concepts—taste and flavours. Now, their thoughts start to shift from their stomach to their tongue as they learn that the food that they are eating can be made more interesting by using it.

After the beautiful experiences of new tastes and flavours, they explore the next level of luxury—ambience. Their surroundings teach them about the luxury that they are experiencing right now. They could be upgraded to the next level if they can add ambience in addition to the tastes and flavours in their life. At this point, their thoughts move from the tongue to the mind. When they start enjoying this pleasure, the brain drives their journey. Now, they just need to sustain the things that they have achieved.

Migrants come to major cities from all parts of the country. They come with the primary agenda of survival and encash the opportunity available in the new place. Their numbers are pretty significant compared to the inhabitants. Because of the migrants, local people have to share their resources and job opportunities. Residents must put more rigorous effort into doing similar things, which they could access pretty comfortably before the arrival of these unwanted guests. Naturally, it creates a sense of insecurity and a feeling of competition among them. Apart from the shortage of jobs and resources, migrants bring in a new way of life. This includes culture, food and communication habits, provoking the residents into thinking that they are damaging their traditions.

Overall, it creates a tense atmosphere and challenges for the migrants. Somewhere, a feeling of inferiority complex develops in them. But in the initial stages, migrants are not very interested in the competition since they struggle with meeting the basic necessities. They come with their dreams and desires, sacrificing the company of their loved ones. They start to work hard to attain their priorities and are prepared to pay any price to achieve this.

With time, they learn that things would be easy if they look like the locals and adapt their lifestyles. So, keeping their goals in mind, they start transforming everything that would make them look like the locals.

They begin to laugh at the jokes that people around them find funny, celebrate with their colleagues, adopt the tone of their language, their clothes and all the millions of things that they feel differentiate them from the people around them. In this process, they have to suppress their original deep-rooted character, which took several years to develop and is even bonded with their DNA. This new character acts as a coating on their unique personality. With this, they become successful in fitting into their contemporary society. But after a while, as they begin to meet their essential requirements, their thoughts shift from their stomach toward their mind and heart.

At this moment of transformation, they realise that they are different now. They discover that their original character is different from the newly developed one in thought and action.

Now, they are stuck between their two personas, of which, one was nurtured by their parents in an atmosphere that included blessings from their ancestors, while the other was developed with the motive to survive.

In all this struggle, they re-evaluate the factors that make them who they are because they sacrificed their native place and customs, taking on the opportunities, bright future and other positive elements in the new place. Unfortunately, every time, their heart takes the side of their native home while their mind tries to justify the present scenario. But the heart always cries like a small child who does not understand the logic and rules of this world. It would not go into an in-depth process of weighing the benefits of the decisions taken. Some part of the heart is always engaged with pleasant memories. They miss everything that actually belongs to them, with which they lived the most remarkable moments of their lives. It develops a feeling of loneliness. This loneliness occupies a permanent place and always gives them a sense of having lost a battle. Like somewhere, something is missing!

During my site visits, I interacted with many people and was often involved in team building, training and successful project completion parties. Most of the time when I was on tours, after office hours, I didn't have anything to do; hence I never resisted all these, which in turn increased my social circle. Whenever I was on tours, all these became my only source of entertainment. I kind of started to like the moments when the real world diminished a bit and my virtual world gained more and more reality.

Within a few months, different groups formed, which did not even require a reason for holding any event. As soon as I reached a particular site, we met and planned a gathering. We smoked, drank a lot and fooled ourselves into thinking we were successful and enjoying our life to the fullest. We never realised the consequences of all these at that time.

Due to continuous pressure from dad and mom to 'complete' our family and as part of the plan made by Supriya and me (before we shifted here), we decided to have one more baby and hence, Asha was born. With Asha, Supriya got even busier than ever. She continued doing her office work from home even during her pregnancy. But I did not see Supriya paying less attention to both of you because of her work, even once. She always managed to provide everything a child would need. I remember, during weekends, you joined swimming practice, dance workshops, tennis class, etc. because of her effort. I was barely able to contribute because of my busy office schedule.

This schedule continued for a while; I soon reached a saturation level with my professional life and the fake parties. Now, partying with my colleagues was no longer fun. This satiation only stopped me from attending the social gatherings, because

I eventually started doing all this alone. When I sat alone, most of the time, I recalled the old days at my native place. With all this, the urge to return to my native place got stronger. You know all these things work like a chain reaction. They tend to grow exponentially.

I always remembered my early life with mom, dad and Supriya and started to compare it with my current lifestyle. This was when the idea of 'Ghar Vapsi' came to mind.

Things I missed the most about my home town:

* In the morning, I wanted to water my small garden, crush the tulsi leaves with my fingers and smell them. I wanted to have tea with my parents on our tiny balcony, encircled by the small plants.

* I aspired to laugh with my mouth wide open till my stomach hurt at the clumsy jokes of my parents or friends. The jokes I heard here were funny but did not touch me. They did not stir me and I often laughed to show support to the other person, even when I did not want to.

* I wanted to mimic my mother's actions; she used to run after me. I always ran intending to be caught and she always saw me with the intention of forgiveness.

* I wanted to sit on the low wall constructed around the trees at our road junction and discuss nonsense with my friends. The issues I discussed here often did not reflect what was inside me, what I usually thought about. These topics were influenced by this new world.

* I wanted my children to experience the fun of flying kites on the rooftop in the full sun, run barefoot in the loose

soil of a freshly cultivated farmland, taste the array of dew droplets accumulated on leaves and feel the sweet pain of touching sugarcane leaves while running between them, convince the local shopkeeper to start a new account, search for the ball with friends in muddy bushes and block the water in the muddy channel before it entered the farmland.

* For the first 30 years of my life, I learned about the husband-wife relationship by watching my parents. They used to fight, but every time, they magically revealed their feelings of love for each other unconsciously. I missed every single second of those precious moments.

* Everything about my hometown was my favourite—I was friends with not just people my age but even those of my parent's generation; like with the shopkeeper uncle who sometimes gave us a bar of free chocolate; after seeing a roadside dog, we would run inside the kitchen and bring biscuits for him; the summer wind under which we used to play cricket; the school where we learned the first lesson of our life; the street where we could play the whole day without being exhausted.

But somewhere, I knew this plan was impossible to execute. I had to wind up all the ongoing tasks here, like completing your education and then accumulating enough funds for our future, as well as convince Supriya. I often tried to discuss this with her, but she always replied casually. She would smile or say, "We will see in the future."

I started working on my plan independently and hard. At this point, my real character (which developed during my childhood) began to dominate and liquidate the coating formed here. As a result, all the things I felt comfortable with here started to feel unusual. I did not want to smile anymore at the fake jokes, discuss unwanted topics and do millions of other things. I stopped attending my office parties. All these feelings inside me began to develop exponentially. I was hardly able to concentrate on my professional or personal life.

When you are busy at the office or at home, this loneliness becomes more acute because no one knows how you feel inside. It is depressing to see people going about their business, not knowing that someone within reach is hurting so much inside.

It is an unusual type of loneliness. This is not a periodical one. It is not a loneliness that crawls up and puts its hands on your shoulder while you are doing something. This is a constant feeling that grips you every waking and sleeping moment. It is a loneliness that restricts the blood flowing to and from your heart when you share your most profound feelings, only to have them ignored or slandered.

No one can forget the place where they were born and brought up. In the process of growing old, whatever we experience and witness leaves an impression on our minds. The effect of this impact is impossible to remove. It is like your own scent that proves your uniqueness and presence. We search for a similar atmosphere around us when we move into a new place, which is natural and expected. Not just in humans, it happens with animals and plants too. Usually, migrated plants and animals cannot survive and fall sick in their new habitat. So, to keep them alive, we need to simulate different natural scenarios (similar conditions to their native places). With these simulations, they manage to withstand the new environment and God alone knows about their happiness.

Chapter 7.7

The Dream of Phoenix (Letter from Dad)

A glacier develops its size over many years until a piece splits off and moves away from it. This newly-born piece of ice is very agile in nature. After separation, it feels free, passionate and full of desire. Sometimes it looks towards the glacier with a grim feeling, often questioning its ability, about why it is so dead slow and tedious.

This little piece of ice cannot figure out the calmness and stability behind the tedious nature. It has minimal knowledge about the deep and vast values that its parent glacier holds within. This piece of ice still needs time to develop its thought process so that it can diagnose any situation or character more thoroughly.

There is another vital quality that we need to develop. We do not have any right to declare anything wrong or unethical if it is beyond our understanding. It is not at all mandatory to colour everything with our point of view. People have a habit of judging everything.

A piece of ice can never be denied because it is a part of the glacier, even if it attains another size, shape or speed in the future. Its every action and decision somewhere contain the impact of the parent glacier.

Each generation is born from the previous one and, in every circumstance, looks to its parents' generation for guidance. As the younger generation matures, it evolves its sense of identity. During the initial phase of the evolution, these newcomers compare their parents with the atmosphere of the instantaneous outside world. Because of their underdeveloped skills in analysing circumstances, they begin to form a negative impression of their parents for a while.

And that is absolutely not the fault of the young ones. This is because everything is driven by an elusive reality in this modern world.

A whole new world is being designed. In this world, different scenarios are created which are attractive and desired by everyone. Millions of advanced technologies and mind games are used to manipulate things. Research is being done on how we can make those virtual things seem more real. Skills are being developed to enlarge the profitable side of a product and hide the undesirable one. For example, nowadays, people are more attracted to a camera capable of creating a good photo of them. Please do not misunderstand; they do not want technology replicating their real picture. Instead, they want a camera that should be equipped with some artificial intelligence to process the captured image and produce a glamorous photo of them. This photo does not resemble the actual person but is accepted by the mind without question.

The camera company does not launch these illusive cameras directly into the market. Initially, they invest huge amounts of money in training our minds, which teaches us the different parameters for accepting and rejecting anything. They define their own set of parameters for deciding what is beautiful and what is ugly. Then, they link that acceptance and rejection with an individual's social status. All of us continuously undergo this training without any control over it or ourselves. Cinema and digital media are advanced aspects of their training faculty. Initially, they project some unreal situations and imaginary characters perform in a hypothetical scenario. Then, they finally present it to us by wrapping everything in an emotionally appealing packaging. Later, the whole market tries to sell these packages to the real world.

This complicated process of evolution eventually separates the child from the parents, the younger generation from the older ones and the chunk of ice from the glacier.

In this hypnotised state, the piece of ice floats away from its roots into this virtual world with a dream that one day it will grow into a glacier with enhanced properties (much more prominent in size, brighter and more colourful) than its parent. But to some extent, this separation also affects the older generation. Somewhere, they know that their children will never return from this journey. Still, they do not want their wishes to obstruct their children's ride. For their own relief, they justify these moves by emphasising words like 'freedom,' 'independence,' and 'modernisation' while communicating with their children or with the people around them.

The harsh truth is that this virtual worldview is weakening us daily. Everyone wants everything in a perfect form, not in the real one. Do you know why?

Because natural is not attractive and comfortable. It often brings some other undesirable components with itself. We manipulate these real and naturally occurring things with technology, wrap them with modernisation and make them perfect. This perfection is good-looking, instant and comfortable. But, because of this, with every passing day, we lose our capability to accept what is real.

Natural relations, happiness, pain, sweetness or sourness can never exist naturally in a perfect form. Even when we visit a market, we expect the fruits and vegetables to be in perfect shape, size, colour and taste. Thousands of companies accept it as a responsibility, set up an industry and provide this to us by adding different chemicals in the form of chemical fertilisers, coating to give shine and sometimes even artificial colouring.

My problem is not with this label of new generation or with the small piece of ice. My problem is not with the desire to grow further or to dream of a better tomorrow. It is with not understanding the exact characteristics of the glacier, developing an inferior impression of our parents or losing control over our minds due to these different strategies all around us.

The real problem starts when we lose the purity in our relationship with our parents, when the exchange of feelings and emotions stops completely. Due to the narrowness of our thought process, we create a crack in our strong bonds that could have lasted forever and the cracks cannot be glued back even with our efforts at recovery. A perfect setting for self-destruction begins to form when the piece of ice loses confidence in the glacier.

It cannot be denied that the motive, desires, dreams and other aspirations change with each new generation. It will be complete injustice if we compare the situation between two different ages, but there is one thing we cannot forget—it is all ice. At the end of the day, we share our DNA with our parents. The relationship between parents and children is naturally bonded with emotional, biological and chemical connections and undoubtedly, they are an essential part of our life.

There were rare moments when I had to travel with Ajay for official work. His profile was related to testing; hence, he often worked from the office. However, I dealt with the implementation of the project, which included frequent travelling.

Once, due to some confusion, there was an escalation raised by one of our reputed clients based in Bangalore. Hence, the company decided to send both of us there.

We were very excited to convert this official trip into an adventure. We had to stay there for around 8–10 days. Because of my frequent trips to this city, I was pretty familiar with the people and the places. So, I arranged a car through one of my colleagues there. After our office hours, every day, we used to visit the famous places there—mostly bars and pubs. After having a good time, we would return to our hotel, usually between 11 to 12, most of the time in a completely drunken state. We followed the same routine nearly every day.

One night, we were returning from one of the famous beer breweries, where they serve craft beer with loud Bollywood music, at around 11:30 pm. Ajay received a call from a landline number with the area code for Lucknow. We were startled to see a call from Lucknow at that time of the night. I immediately stopped the car on one side of the road while Ajay picked up the phone. It was quiet, so I could hear parts of their conversation. Ajay's mom was on the other side and was explaining something. I could figure out the panic in her voice. Eventually, Ajay's expression changed from bad to worse. After a few minutes, he hung up the phone and stared at me with a puzzled expression. That evening, we both had a lot to drink and were relatively high.

He said, "That was my mother... She told me that dad had a minor chest pain for the last 4–5 days. Since this morning, it has become unbearable, so they visited the hospital for a medical check-up. The doctor performed some examinations. The report came just now and the doctor advised bypass surgery urgently since 90% of his arteries are blocked. He has a high risk of heart failure or a major stroke. But dad is refusing emergency surgery, as he wants to meet all of us before entering the operation theatre. Mom is panicking because she is alone and unable to decide what to do. She called *mama* (uncle) from Kanpur; he will reach there by tomorrow morning."

"Don't worry, I will ask my parents to go to the hospital," I said taking the cell phone from Ajay's hand. I called my home and informed dad about the situation. The hospital was very close to my house. After hanging up, I asked Ajay to talk to his father and convince him that he would reach Lucknow by the next evening and to proceed with the surgery. Somehow, Ajay's mom arranged a cell phone in the hospital. Ajay had a long conversation with his father. His father repeatedly said that he would die soon, so he wanted to meet everyone before that. Finally, Ajay convinced him that they would all reach Lucknow by the next afternoon while the doctor made preparations for the surgery. After meeting with Ajay, he would proceed with the surgery immediately.

While Ajay was talking with his father, I realised the significance of every passing second, so I started the car and began to drive towards our hotel. While Ajay finished his conversation, I parked the car outside the hotel. I told him we should immediately check out from the hotel and reach the airport with our luggage. I told him to take a flight to Lucknow or Delhi (whichever was available) while I go to Bombay, pick up his family and take them to Lucknow on a train. Ajay was not responding and looked very tense, just shaking his face at my every suggestion. Without wasting any time, we checked out of the hotel. Then, we proceeded to hand over the car to my colleague and took a taxi to the airport.

Meanwhile, I informed my boss about this emergency. On reaching the airport and inquiring about flights, we discovered that there were no flights at night. Even on the next day, no trip to Lucknow was scheduled, but the next day at 7.30 am, one flight to Delhi was available and at 10.00 am to Bombay. We had no other options, so we purchased tickets for both flights.

Then, I called my travel agent in Bombay to book train tickets from Bombay to Lucknow for me and Ajay's family and a Delhi to Lucknow flight for Ajay. Luckily, the travel agent answered the phone and I gave him all the traveller details with the train options.

Within half an hour, the travel agent confirmed the booking of our tickets. "Sir, tomorrow I will send the tickets to your email ID and you can take a printout in some cyber cafe outside the railway station," he said.

Now, it was time to call Supriya. I called on our landline and as it was 12.50 am, she answered the phone with some hesitation. I told her about the whole incident and our travel plans. "So, tomorrow, I will reach Bombay at one in the afternoon and we will catch a train to Lucknow at 4.30 pm from Bombay Central. There will be a marginal time difference, so I will go directly from the airport to the railway station. You explain everything to Sheetal Bhabhi, pack some clothes for me and hand them over to her. If possible, spend some time with her; she may require your support," I said and hung up.

While I was managing all this, it was already 1.30 am. As Ajay had an early-morning flight, we decided to go to the airport waiting room and planned to take some rest there. We kept our luggage on one of the foldable semi-sleeper chairs and freshened up in the bathroom in the waiting area. Ajay looked very disturbed and asked me to sit in the airport bar for a while. It was just in front of the waiting room, so we went there and chose to sit at a corner table. There was a big glass window from which there was a beautiful view of Bangalore city. Thousands of glittering lights were visible from there. I ordered two large whiskys while Ajay continuously looked toward those lights without blinking his eyes.

After a few minutes of silence, I stood next to him, put my hand on his shoulders and said, "Don't worry, Ajay, everything will be fine." Teardrops rolled out of his eyes and hung on his chin. I handed him the whisky with some tissues. He gulped it down in one shot and continued to stare outside the window. After a few moments, he broke the silence.

"Don't you think we travelled too far from where we started? Don't you feel that the kind of bond we used to share with our family is getting weaker with every passing second? It looks like everything is becoming dull in the bright light around us. For the last few years, I have felt strongly that I am going through something very unnatural, but I'm not able to identify it. The most worrying thing, I think, about today's incident is that I absolutely did not have any clue about my dad's pain even though I talk to him almost daily. Can you imagine any child suffering from a problem for 2 or 3 days whose parents don't come to know about it, even if the child does not share it with them? Ultimately, it's my responsibility to take care of my parents, to figure out the requirement for any medical check-up or the hundred other things that have to be taken care of, just like they used to do for me when I was a child. Honestly, I talk to them like it was a task assigned to me and do not even remember what we discussed after an hour since my heart and feelings are not involved. And this works both ways; even my parents have no idea about the significant pain I am going through or what my family is dealing with. Don't you think this violates some of a family's essential requirements? Even when we visit Lucknow, we do it like some guests who have come to accomplish some task or purpose."

This was the first time that Ajay discussed this portion of his life with me. It shocked me, as it resembled the feelings I had been going through for the last few months. But somewhere, it gave me a tiny sense of relief; I was not going through anything abnormal. For sure, in this situation, I did not want to open my bag of pain in front of him since he was already worried about his father's operation. I took the glass from his hand, cleared the bill, took him to the waiting room to our chair and told him to rest for a while since the next day was going to be very hectic for both of us.

The next morning, we left on schedule. I reached the Bombay Central railway station, where I found Sheetal Bhabhi with her daughter. An hour and a half remained for the train's scheduled departure. Thankfully, Supriya had sent some food for me. I had been starving since morning, but the best part about this journey was that it would continue for the next 32 hours. So, I would get ample time to take rest. I called Ajay to confirm his status and he told me that he had caught his flight to Lucknow on schedule.

Finally, we reached Lucknow and took an auto to Ajay's house. I saw many people gathered outside his house as we entered his lane. On entering his home, we heard the sound of many women crying. An uncle informed us that Ajay's father had passed away the previous evening during his bypass surgery. Everybody had just left for the funeral ceremony at the riverfront. I placed my luggage in one of the rooms and while exiting the room saw Ajay's mother sitting at the centre of the house with many other women gathered around her. Everybody was crying and I made eye contact with his mother. Her eyes were swollen and she looked toward me for a moment like she wanted to share something, but then she covered her face with her sari.

I borrowed a bike from his neighbours and drove towards the riverfront. When I reached there, I found that around 5–6 bodies were burning and each one was surrounded by many people. This was the first time I had ever come to this place. After a few minutes of inquiry and searching, I managed to find Ajay. Around 7–8 people were standing around him and his father's body was almost burnt. It looked like most of the people had already left. When Ajay saw me, he hugged me and started crying loudly. People came forward to calm him down.

Meanwhile, the priest called Ajay for some pooja and other rituals. The prayers and rituals continued for another half an hour till the body was cremated completely. Everybody began to leave and they asked Ajay to go with them. But he came to me and murmured, "Ask everyone to go, as I want to stay here for a while. Tell them that I will go with you."

Somehow, I convinced everyone and assured them that I would take care of him and bring him home safely within an hour. Then we sat on the river bank, the sand was wet and the weather was freezing compared to Bombay. The river water sporadically touched our feet. In the background, mantras were being chanted and bells and the hushed sounds of random people crying could be heard. The sun was going down and our shadows were getting darker and longer with every passing second. We were sitting in complete silence staring at the *diyas* floating in the river. They travelled for some distance and then disappeared as they sank beneath the river waves.

I kept my arm around Ajay's shoulder. I wanted to break the silence but did not know what to say or how to say it. After a while, I gathered courage and said in a low voice, "Don't worry,

Ajay, that's the harsh truth of nature; nobody has any option but to accept it."

Ajay did not react in any way. After a few moments, however, he smiled a bit, threw a small piece of stone into the water and said, "You know, as an ex-serviceman, my father was very strict, just the opposite of my mom. I was terrified of his angry eyes. Seriously, his strong voice would make me wet my pants. I hated school and studies. I was horrible at academics and always scared of exams. One day, when I was in the 7th standard, dad came to pick me up. He used to randomly come to my school to drop me off or to take me home. When I reached the main gate, I saw him standing there. Coincidentally, my class test results had come out that day and I had failed. My class teacher told me to get it signed by my parents. I used to manage all these with mom. Dad hardly knew about these monthly tests. When I saw him, tears streamed down my face. Dad saw the tears, was shocked and began to question me. Without overthinking, I held my stomach and told him that I'd been going through a stomach ache for the last hour. He immediately took me to a nearby hospital. The doctor gave me some basic medicines. While we were returning home, dad asked me, 'Why didn't you inform your teachers about this?' Without thinking about the consequences, I replied, 'I did tell her about this, but she asked me to have some water and that it will be okay.' Now, dad was furious. For the rest of the way, he kept talking about my teacher and how they could be so irresponsible. He also mentioned that the next day, he would come to the school and complain to my principal about this. After this, I was uneasy and I had no idea how to handle the situation. So, as soon as we reached home, I explained the whole situation to mom. Initially, she laughed a lot, but then she promised me that she would handle it without letting dad find out anything. And like all the other times, her incredible skills saved me from that situation.

There was a time when my teachers used to say that I could never complete high school. I was so weak in academics that I failed two times before I finished high school, in classes 9th and 11th. Undoubtedly, dad loved me a lot but never showed his love directly. It always remained hidden behind his robust demeanour. He was determined to give direction to my future. He is the only reason that I became capable of completing my post-graduation and managing my family today. You know, until I completed my graduation, the relationship between dad and me was very brittle. But the moment I moved to Bombay for my MBA, there was a drastic change in his behaviour. Eventually, his tough outer layer started to vaporise. He never missed an opportunity to talk to me on the telephone and our conversations sometimes extended up to hours. Or when I visited here, we used to sit and discuss everything under the sun. This sort of discussion was never a part of our routine when living together. But once I moved away, he would discuss his daily routine, his conversation with his friends and his financial plans. Most of the time, these conversations were meaningless, but he wanted to share each and every part of his life. Many times, mom told me that he missed me a lot. But from the moment I shifted here, I was surrounded by tasks. One after the other, some or the other thing was always pending, even if I tried to keep pace. All the time, I was hoping that once things were settled, I could spend more time with mom and dad, but it never happened. And look, ultimately, the worst has happened.

Before he entered the operation theatre, I talked to him for about fifteen minutes. And you will be surprised to know his last words. He said, 'A relationship has a tendency to neither build up nor get over in a moment. It requires continuous nourishment for years to grow and millions of wounds to end.'

A relationship isn't necessarily finished if someone dies or stops talking to you. But subsequently, it loses all its worth if the people involved lose affection for each other and stop sharing their thoughts regularly. At that moment, a relationship has died a death of a thousand cuts. At this moment, the primary feeling of guilt in my heart is the millions of things that remain unsaid between us. I can't deny that for the last 1–2 years, whatever relationship I had with my parents was very formal. Somewhere, that closeness was missing."

With this, Ajay could not hold back his tears and started to cry like a small child. I let him cry for a while and tried my best to rein my tears. After a time, when he calmed down, I hugged him tightly and breathed into his ears, "I can understand, dear."

I then asked Ajay to return home as everybody was waiting for us. On our way to Ajay's house, millions of thoughts were flitting across my mind. These were the same thoughts that frightened me most of the time. I had always heard that time is mighty, but at that moment, I felt the real power it held. Two days ago, at this time, we were returning from a bar. Ajay was drunk and roaring while sticking his head out of the car's window like some unstoppable bull. We were discussing our plans to buy a house or upgrade our vehicle. But now, he was crying like a child, holding my shirt with both his hands. His head and shoulders were bowed down like he had lost everything today. Just imagine the unpredictable variable factors present behind every situation, but we often dare to think that every situation is under control.

It was around 11.00 pm when we reached home. Dad was standing at the main entrance of Ajay's home. I indicated that I would be back in a moment after taking Ajay inside the house. Ajay did not see him. We saw his mother and wife sitting inside upon entering his room.

I left him there. Then, I came outside to meet dad, touch his feet and sit on the plastic chair near the main gate. I explained everything to him. I told him that Ajay was very disturbed, so it would be better if I stayed with him that night. I asked him not to worry and that I would come late at night after he was asleep or the next morning. Dad took a small tiffin box out of his side bag and said, "No need to hurry. Just be with Ajay. Mom has sent some food for you. Share it with him. Maybe he hasn't had anything to eat for a long time."

I just looked at him, hugged him and whispered in his ears, "I love you, Dad." I am not sure if he heard that. Seriously, our parents know us far better than we can even imagine. They just preserve all those memories we spend with them and live their life cherishing them.

I said goodbye to him and proceeded toward Ajay's room. He was sitting alone. I told him that mom had sent some food for him. Initially, he refused to eat but then agreed and we shared the tiffin. While eating, he said, "I will always be thankful to you for all your help. Seriously, I might not have been able to spend those precious last moments with my father if you hadn't supported me."

I looked at him and replied, "We are living there, away from our parents and relatives. My family survives because of your support, so it would be an insult to me if you thank me again."

He asked me to sleep in his room as it was already 1.30 am and I was dead tired. The last three days were a lot to take and above the physical tiredness, I just wanted to pause my mind for a while. Finally, I went to bed.

Closing my eyelids made me feel that ages had passed since I had laid down to rest. Very soon, I entered deep sleep. After a while, I opened my eyes, sensing some disturbance. It was completely dark. I could make out the outline of a large bird sitting at the foot of my bed. As I looked more closely, it resembled an eagle, except it was a bit different and bigger than I was used to seeing.

I tried to get up from my bed, but I had to exert enormous effort. I felt fragile, my hands were trembling and my feet stumbled as they touched the ground. Finally, leaning on my bed, I stood up. It was a very tiring process. There was a large mirror just in front of my bed and as I looked at it, I was horrified. My hair was white and I could see two prominent bones under my eyes. It was an older man, aged 70–75 years.

I could not see much as I turned around, but I started to scan the place. The dark shadow of nearby objects began to take shape. This place resembled my room in Lucknow, but it looked very untidy. I had never seen my room in such bad shape. There were layers of dust all over, cobwebs everywhere, the furniture was covered with bedsheets, layers of paint were peeling off the walls and broken glass from the windows was lying on the floor. In many places, the floor tiles were broken and vegetation grew in those cracks.

Meanwhile, the bird spread its broad wings and started to fly. There was a cloud of dust produced in its wake. Then, it turned around and looked at me, making eye contact with me, like instructing me to follow it with its sharp and pointed eyes.

As I followed it outside, I could see much better. Now I was sure that this was my Lucknow house, but looking at the condition of the house, it appeared that nobody had been staying here for years. As I was walking, the loose floor tiles cracked under my feet.

The bird continued to fly towards our porch. I started to follow it like I was hypnotised by it. The chairs and tables were broken and pieces were lying all over the floor. The whole area was surrounded by pots with dead plants, the soil inside them dried up and cracked. The bird then sat on the railing and flashed a white light on the front wall, just like a projector. Some blurred images emerged, showing pictures from when I was a kid, around 4–5 years old. Mom and dad were sitting on the chairs and having tea, I was playing around them. While I was running, I accidentally hit mom's chair from behind. Since mom had a cup of tea in her hand, it spilled and spread all over the table and floor. Immediately, she ran after me, shouting. To defend myself, I ran fast. Dad loudly cheered me to run faster so that mom could not catch me. Unfortunately, mom grabbed me. She pinched my ear and while I was screaming, she pulled me towards the table and asked me to bring a cloth to clean the spilled tea. As I turned to get the cloth, dad playfully splashed the tea on the table towards mom and ran, lifting me on his way out. Mom shouted even louder and ran behind us. After some distance, she caught up with both of us and then a volley of laughter erupted. The whole house was filled with the echoes of our laughter. Within a few seconds, that white light disappeared.

The bird started to fly again. I followed it into the living room, where there was a strong, damp smell. I reached the dining table and as I touched it, it collapsed. The bird settled down just in front of me, near two dead bodies lying on the floor, covered with a dusty-toned black cloth. The bird flapped its wings, uncovering the fabric from the face of both the bodies. It was mom and dad. My clothes were completely wet with sweat and I was shivering. I sat on the floor like all the energy had drained out of my body. I was looking at them with my eyes wide open. Their faces seemed very expressive and full of emotions. I could still see some sort of restlessness in their expression.

The bird then started to fly and as it reached the roof, it stopped and started projecting images again. These were pictures of the room where mom and dad were lying on the floor and both were in pain. They were chanting the name of every family member with their fumbling voice. Mom was continuously asking about all of us.

Meanwhile, dad tried to convince her, "Don't worry, they will all come soon. Do you even know how far Bombay is from here?"

But mom was repeating the same thing.

This time, dad replied, "Our son has become very successful now, always surrounded by glittering objects. Recently, they purchased a brand-new car. You know, none of our relatives have ever purchased such an expensive car. They are even planning to buy a house there. Our children make us proud in the whole society and Supriya also got promoted last month. She has now become the head of the Bombay branch. We are so lucky to have a family like this."

Mom interrupted, "I don't understand all this. For me, things were much easier when he was a kid and less intelligent than this. At least he trusted my feelings and had confidence in my choices. Even when he used to have any doubts, I could make him understand by pulling his ears."

But dad started talking about us again, "Our grandchildren are studying in world-class schools."

Mom interrupted him, "So that means our grandchildren will also move far away from their parents. Oh, God! Please slow down the growth of our family and limit our grandchildren's success within reach of their family."

Mom turned towards dad and stared into his eyes. Dad also paused and froze. After a few minutes of silence, they hugged each other and started crying loudly. They supported each other's heads with their hands and their echoing breaths were clearly audible. The immortal curtain seemed to rise before their last few breaths. In their final moments, mom raised her radiant head in front of dad's face, looked into his eyes, wiped down his tears, kissed him on his forehead and then returned to her original position. Eventually, the echoing breaths stopped and everything dissolved into a deep, dark silence.

Meanwhile, I could feel somebody shaking me hard. I opened my eyes and the first thought that came to my mind was "Oh damn! It was a dream."

I was sweating profusely and it took me a few seconds to realise that it was a dream and not an actual incident. My heart was pounding. I wanted to pacify myself with a glass of water, but all this had left me weak and trembling and 6–7 people, including Ajay, were all around my bed. Ajay was standing just in front of me. He handed me a glass of water and said, "You okay, *na*? While sleeping, you were shivering very badly and shouting out at times." I just held my head and sat on the floor. While looking at everyone, I said, "I am sorry, it was just a bad dream. You can all sleep."

I cannot explain how relieved I felt at that moment, considering it was all a dream. That dream was one of the most horrible experiences of my life. I did not want to recall it again, but surprisingly, even after returning to Bombay, the dream kept haunting me.

Chapter 7.8

The Last Wish (Letter from Dad)

I have so many emotions inside me that I want to share with all of you. At this moment, I feel lucky to have a family like you. I love you all.

And finally, I want you all to know that I did not fail in my life, I fought every situation putting in my best effort, but yes, I could not manage the risk assessment of my life. I kept doing computations of profits and losses for the risks that could be dropped or delayed. I did not identify the most momentous risk that could occur, which seals everything—*My life itself*.

It is my last wish that all of you move to our house in Lucknow immediately. I will come there once to meet you all for the last time.

Chapter 08

The Ultimate Vapsi

When we finished reading the letter, none of us moved. Tears stained my face, my eyes were dull, my skin was pale and my hair was messed up. I seriously wanted this letter to go on forever. It made me feel like I was talking to dad and he was acknowledging my questions. Oh! It could not be finished now. I still had thousands of questions unanswered.

Mom was sitting next to me. She began to shake her legs and then stumbled onto the bed. Dadi sat behind her, supported her and gave her a glass of water. While mom, dada and I finished reading the letter, dadi and Asha (sitting on dadi's lap) stared at us with millions of questions in their eyes, but they did not ask anything. Dada and dadi tried their best to control their emotions and not cry in front of us.

I placed my head on mom's lap and started crying loudly. She put her hands on my head and said with tears in her eyes, "But how could he withhold such a major part of his life from me? This is pure dishonesty. I shared every pain in my life with him and everything was equal between us. How could he even think of living alone with so much pain inside him? I was so stupid to have had no idea about this."

Mom then turned towards dada and continued, "If he had revealed all those things, we could have tried to sort things out and the disease could have been tackled with the best doctors in the world." At this moment, the last line of the letter flashed in my mind. I said emphatically, "We should move to Lucknow as soon as possible. You remember the last line written by dad?"

Within an hour, we locked our house and, without taking much luggage with us, took a taxi to the airport. As we reached the airport, dada enquired about the latest flight to Lucknow at all the airline counters. Luckily, the next flight was just after two hours.

When we were waiting in front of the gate, Asha came to me and asked, "But why did Dad not come with us? Couldn't we have gone there together? And why are we going to Lucknow when Dada and Dadi are still here?" I hugged her and said, "Maybe he has planned some big surprise for us." Tears rolled down my eyes and I was hoping that what I said to her would turn out to be true.

Finally, we reached Lucknow and each of us was looking for dad in every possible place. When we arrived home, dada started making inquiries at the house of neighbours before entering the house. But none of them had any clue about dad.

For the next four days, we searched all the possible places in Lucknow, including hospitals, markets and police stations, talked to all of his friends and went to every place dad knew. But we did not find any trace of him. On the 5th day, in the morning, at around ten, we had just finished our breakfast and were sitting at the dining table. The doorbell rang.

I opened the door to find two men aged 40–45 years standing at the door in hospital uniforms. Then I noticed an ambulance parked just in front of our main entrance. The men confirmed dada's name and then turned to call two more people from the ambulance to open its back door. They dragged a stretcher out of the ambulance with a body covered with a white bedsheet.

My heart stopped beating and I froze. Somehow, I managed to reach the stretcher and collected my courage to remove the bedsheet to identify the face... And *it was Dad.*

I laid my head on his chest and touched his lips. His body was cold and I lightly moved my fingers on his face. One of the men from the hospital announced, "Ashok Singhal."

I sat down on my knees in the middle of the road, bowed my head and started crying. While they were moving the stretcher towards the house, I could hear the loud sound of screaming coming from dada, dadi and mom.

Dad's body was placed in the centre of the outer lawn. We were sitting around him, crying and sobbing. I could see his unresponsive body lying on the grass, the warmth of his life stolen by cruel desires, but it could not touch the innocence of his face. He had never imagined this kind of Ghar Vapsi for himself. The house's front wall was occupied by birds as if they were showing their gratitude in return for the food and water they consumed.

The Last Page

- The beginning is always optimistic and full of promises. We believe in the strong wings of dreams and have expectations of a golden future. We are driven by the force of desire.

- The middle is always engaging, and scattered, constantly pushing us to reach targets and deadlines and we are in a hurry to finish.

- The end is always incomplete but full of opportunities to explore new possibilities and invent better directions for the future. Its outcome could be desirable or undesirable, but it is always based on the harsh reality of the world. This outcome is always free from all illusions.

There are no perfect happy endings in real life. The conclusions permanently remove all the layers of our misconceptions and beliefs based on imaginary thoughts. They always stand on harsh realities.

Here, I conclude my message, hoping for a pleasing start that we will come out of our imaginary world. Break the baseless belief. In the beginning, it could be a challenge to face real things in this real world, but it will improve the result in the end, which is what really matters in the end.

We are not here to justify or to protect our social/religious/caste/regional identities. These tags, with their set of rules, are based on lies. We can only understand the difference between a truth and a lie if we analyse them, leaving the past behind and then forgetting the tags assigned by ourselves based on the constant influence of society. We need to raise questions against them.

What if someone disagrees with our religious rituals?

We can withdraw from any discussions even if we think we are right. We could be proven wrong, even if we are more powerful and wealthy than the person we are arguing with. We can easily forget the bitter part of any relationship.

Even if we disagree or have trouble digesting millions of questions like these, there can be many constructive ways to express ourselves.

When we meet someone, based on their name, physical appearance, impression, or point of view, thousands of other assumptions are made by us. This works both ways. Whatever designation or teachings this society based on religion, caste, region and family has given to us, we take it as a responsibility to justify its workings.

* It is important to perform a precise risk assessment of our life since it will decide how much effort we need to put in, the money we need to earn and to what extent we need to work. It will help us to prioritise tasks in our day-to-day routine. Remember, our life should have a finishing line, which must be achievable too. If all of us die without reaching our finishing line, it will hardly justify our journey and give us a sense of dissatisfaction in the long run.

* If our excessive hard work and busy routine provide professional growth, then we are losing something along the way. We need to identify what it is we are losing. Urgent and immediate action needs to be undertaken to restore the balance. Taking a break, pause or even a demotion is justified if we can maintain a healthy balance in our personal and professional life.

*** The End ***